LOVE
locks
THE SERIES

DHANI EWING

SOUTH BEACH PUBLISHING

Copyright

Dedication

To Martha Lindblom.

I know this book holds a special place in your heart.

DHANI

X

One - Taboo

His face consumes my every waking moment, and when sleeping, visions of him plunge me into terrifying nightmares that shake and rock me emotionally to my core.

Night after night I awoke in tears because he was always just out of reach, a breath away. But I couldn't stop him from falling, leaving me without that last goodbye. I would do anything, risk anything for that chance, to hear him whisper *I love you* one final time. I have to try, or I would live the rest of my life with regret.

Pulled back to the moment, I'd spoken of a taboo subject, one I should know nothing of.

"Nobody will ever know, Father, I swear to you. I've been told there is a way…"

"Enough of this madness, Raven!"

I'm not prepared to be silenced. "…but something tells me you already know what that way is."

As the esteemed and revered leader of our country, my father wields immense power and has forgotten more secrets than most would remember.

"It is forbidden, Raven and I will not indulge you or this line of conversation any further."

I try to reign my emotions in before they erupt into histrionics that would push him further away from agreeing to help me. "I don't care what you say—I can feel him still…" I place my hand over my heart, feeling it beat a little too fast. "It hurts so much."

"*He* is *not* the one, merely a reflection and I implore you to see it for what it is."

It's more than I dare to believe he would admit to, so soon anyway. "You don't know he won't be the same... at least allow me to–"

He holds a finger up to silence me before continuing. "I know more than you credit me with but mark my words; if you insist on stomping down this reckless path, it will be your undoing and place me in a precarious situation if it should ever come to light."

"One last night, that's all I ask and then I can let him go."

"Seeing that face will not help you."

"It is not *that* face, but *his* face."

"You know what I mean, Raven!"

"I have to do this, but I can't without your help."

"He will not think the same or feel the same way, nor will he know who you are, can you handle that?" He blows out his frustration, his cheeks flushed. Control of his temper waned. "Walking this path will only lead to more heartbreak I would not wish for you, so why will you not listen?"

"I never said goodbye, don't you understand how that feels?"

"You speak to me as if I am an idiot, of course I do, and if I had lost your mother that same way, I-I..." He shakes his head, trying to clear the thoughts of losing his wife in such traumatic circumstances "...but trust me, Raven, this man is–"

"Him."

"No, my child..." He speaks with a warm and tender tone. "...He. Is. Not."

"Help me, and I will never ask another thing of you."

"And go against the very laws I vowed to uphold so long before you were born, never."

"I am your daughter, should my happiness not come before those you govern?"

"Those who voted me into office are beloved by your mother and me. We resolved to tell the absolute truth and I will not sacrifice all I have built up and wreck that trust placed in us."

"Am I not more important than them?"

"Not always, Raven, no."

"You're a cruel man." I don't mean it, but his words wound me.

His hand sweeps toward the city beyond the palace gates. "Their punishment for even speaking of what you ask me to sanction would be swift and severe..." He takes a deep breath. "...you are asking me to overlook the very thing we have sworn never to do—we do not interfere with other worlds."

"Please." I drop to my knees and wrap my arms around his legs. Tears sting my eyes, but worse still, with every passing moment, every fibre of my being feels the forced separation from the man I promised to love forever. "You know I love and respect you, Father." I must tread carefully. "I value our ways. I always have but please, I do not ask this lightly, help me."

We are interrupted by the door of the grand chamber swinging open. It strikes the wall with a thud, leaving a dent in delicate plasterwork. The bang from the door echoes about the cavernous room. My beautiful and wise mother surveys the scene then with purpose etched across her face, walks toward us, her robes sweeping the marbled floors giving the impression she floats. I'm always dazzled by her flawless appearance, but I've seen this particular expression on her face only a few times in my life.

With her honey-blonde hair piled high in a classic chignon and lightly dusted makeup that accentuates what is already there in abundance; a sense of refined majesty fills the room—she means business. I'm struck once more that my parents make quite the perfect figureheads. Their outward appearance not only reflects confidence but their kind and compassionate nature within.

"Hello, darling." Father can't hide his love for her. His eyes and the way they shine upon her approach reveal everything.

"Ah, good, I thought I would find you both here. We have urgent matters to discuss."

"If you don't mind, Adriana, we are in the midst of–"

I see the flash of impatience in her green eyes. Nobody silences my mother and walks away unscathed.

She speaks in a high, authoritative tone. "Your only child is crying out to you for help, Phillipe, and you dare to refuse her. Shame on you."

My mother is resourceful and not much passes by without escaping her notice.

"Not right now, Adriana," he snaps, something he would later pay for when they retired to their suite of rooms.

I do not want to be the cause of disharmony in my parents' marriage and try to stem their quarrel before the rot begins. "Mother, it's fine, we are simply talking."

She looks down upon me, benevolence shining from her stare. Lifting my chin gently she ensures I hear what she wants to say and that I do so as an equal. "Get up off the floor this instant, Raven." She tuts and shoots my father a stare that tells of her displeasure. "Begging any man, especially your own father is beneath you." She helps me to my feet, clutching my hand in hers. Then, she focuses again on my father. Being in disgrace with her is not a place anybody would choose to be. Without words and a withering stare, she could cut a person down to size in seconds. But this manner was usually reserved for those who overstepped and failed to see the bigger picture in what she and my father were trying to achieve. "And what do you have to say for yourself, Phillipe?"

"Me?"

"No, not you. I'm talking to the fool standing behind you."

"Adriana, this conversation is between Raven and me."

He is skating on thin ice. "I humbly request you choose your words wisely because seldom in all the years we have been married have I felt such disappointment toward you."

"Mother, you do not need to fight my battles for me. I am simply stating my case, that is all."

"I answer to nobody, Adriana," he replies with great hauteur, "or have you forgotten who I am?"

"*You* are my husband and father to our only child. Any title you hold aside from the aforementioned is of no consequence right now."

I can see him trying to sidestep marital discord. But like her, he can be forthright with his opinions. Neither likes to be challenged. Him as the President of the Republic of the United Kingdom and her, the sainted First Lady, she of beauty and grace; both rule with compassion and hope that as a society we would eventually become more enlightened and leave uncertain and selfish times behind us.

My father had risen quickly within the ranks, voted into office with unheard of majority term after term because the people always came first. I knew this first-hand as my heartfelt plea failed to move him. "I see you have already made your mind up, and whatever I say will make little difference."

"You are quite correct in your analysis, Phillipe, now answer my question."

I feel horrible causing the conflict between them but as much as my parents adore one another, neither will shy away from going to war if they believe their cause supports it.

Father's face is set. "Do you think me blind and deaf, Adriana?"

With a cocked eyebrow, she fires back at him yet speaks with a softened, tender tone. "True love is written in the stars, my darling, and you of all people should know that. Grant this request, I beseech you."

I wonder, how could she already know of my request?

"He is not–"

"I am well aware of who *he* is but tell that to your daughter's grieving heart and the answer shall always remain the same. The heart wants what it wants, it is what makes us human."

"Father, I will never ask another thing of you." He appears to mull my plea. "Allow this one violation to your precious laws and I pledge my life to service as you and mother have done."

"And if I did by some small miracle agree to this madness, how do I know you will return to me?"

Ah, so that's it, I'm still daddy's girl. I think to myself. *He does not want to lose me.* "You know my existence there could cause problems."

Mother squeezes my hand. Her eyes glisten with tears. "Raven will return to us, I am certain, but for her continued happiness, I will forgive her leaving us if she finds happiness elsewhere."

"She is our only child, Adriana."

"Yet she is miserable, what say you now, Phillipe?"

I step in quickly. "I shall return, you have my word."

Father approaches. Tears fill his bright blue eyes. "Raven, you are my world, and I swore the day your mother and I were blessed with your birth that I would do what I could to ensure your happiness..." He takes a quick breath. "...but sometimes life takes a cruel turn we do not anticipate and one we cannot control. You lost your wonderful husband in such tragic circumstances and, well, if I could swap places and bring him back to you, I would."

Mother's eyes are also wet with tears. She too had been devastated when her much loved son-in-law died.

"I know, which is why I felt I could ask this of you."

"Let her go, Phillipe. She does not have a future if she cannot let go of the past."

"I'm trying, Adriana, but I'm terrified of where this could lead to."

She pats his hand. "I feel the same way you do, but Raven is no longer a little girl. She is a grown woman who knows her own mind."

I say a silent prayer and cross my fingers too, just for added luck. For my father to give in would force him to relinquish what makes him the man he is. I wouldn't hate him if he declined my request, but it would leave me more resolved to find my own way across.

"*One* night only, Raven," he decrees, as thunder shakes the grey skies outside. "And make no mistake, if I have to come and fetch you personally, I will." Forked lightning seals his decision and warns me not to betray my so easily offered promise.

I free myself from my mother's grasp. "Thank you." He opens his arms to me. I fall into them, my chest heaving with sobs. "I feel like I'm dying inside, that the air is being squeezed from my lungs and making this journey is the only way I can continue to breathe."

"Oh, my darling, I had no idea it was so bad for you." Mother surrenders to her own emotions. "I should have known."

"He was my life, Mother, the only man I ever loved, and I feel cheated that I never got to say goodbye."

"You must not tell this other who you are or where you are from," Mother warns. Father nods his head in agreement.

"He would never believe me anyway so why would I?"

"Love makes a person do funny things, but you must keep reminding yourself that he is only a mirror of the man you lost."

"I know that, Father." Looking into this other man's eyes and not being able to tell him the truth will test me to my ultimate limit. But I hope seeing a living breathing version of him will ease the crushing pain in my chest. That seeing this other one alive and happy will somehow make my husband's passing bearable.

Kissing the top of my head, father speaks quietly, "Your mother and I will escort you to the gate and ensure you cross safely, but that is all we can do until you signal us to bring you home."

"You don't know how much this means to me." Tears stain my cheeks.

"I cannot stand to witness your suffering." He holds me close. "It hurts me too, so you may go, and with my blessing."

Two - Lightning Strikes

Dalton...

Pulled from a restless sleep, I force my tired eyes to focus on the alarm clock on the bedside cabinet; 01:03am. *Oh, God, no!* I groan because I have an important meeting mid-morning with my team of accountants and disturbed sleep will leave me irritable and unable to concentrate.

I throw the covers back and slip off the bed. *Warm milk will help.* Then I am distracted and the reason for me waking so early is soon apparent.

From the floor to ceiling windows of my penthouse apartment, I gaze in awe as thunder cracks the grey skies wide open allowing bolts of forked lightning to seep through. I watch, transfixed as flashes strike the pavements. Then, a small lone-standing tree across the road catches fire, but I'm so lost in Mother Nature's magnificent display I do nothing but gawp.

Without realising my actions, my fingers on both hands are splayed on the glass. *Dalton.* I hear something, almost a whisper in the wind and my need to be at one with the elements intensifies.

Quickly glancing at the rain-soaked streets below, I note a silence has spread across the usual bustling city. Right now, Liverpool is deathly quiet, deserted, its vibrancy muted by this freak storm. Coming in from nowhere and without warning, it seems partygoers have scattered far and wide; torrential rain sending most rushing for cover or into waiting taxis to ferry them home.

I look to the left as another flash of lightning illuminates Bertie and Bella atop the clock towers on the Royal Liver Building. It's a sight to behold. I feel a flutter in my stomach at seeing the storm clouds swirling above the familiar monument giving it an air of the supernatural, like otherworldly forces were at play.

Once again, I feel an overriding urge to be at one with nature.

Slipping into skinny jeans and an old jumper that clings to my athletic torso, I scour the bedroom for my boots. Finding one under the bed and another in my walk-in wardrobe, I forgot about socks as I'm inclined to do because I'm usually dressed for comfort and wearing trainers. An unmatched pair would have to do. I felt a sense of urgency, so this was no time to worry too much about looking my best.

Passing the mirror, my hair sticks out at every direction. I look like I've jammed my finger in the plug socket. A quick dab of wax onto the palm of my hands sorts the mess, and my light-brown hair quickly looks presentable.

Dalton.

I spin around, certain somebody is standing behind me, but I'm imagining it. I press the elevator call button then realise I've forgotten my contact lenses. Leaving without them in wasn't a good idea, and glasses would be a nightmare in the continuing downpour. I race into my bathroom, put my lenses in and grab my grey wool coat from the cloakroom. I step into my private elevator and hum to myself. Thirty seconds later the doors open into the main reception area of the serviced building.

Forbes, the trusted night Concierge approaches. He checks his gold watch and smiles.

"It is unusual to see you at such a late hour, Mr Delaney."

"Yes, I suppose it is, but I couldn't sleep."

"Would you like me to call your driver?"

"No thank you, Forbes, not tonight."

"Then might I offer to drive you where you wish to go?"

"There will be no need, I just fancy a walk."

"In this weather?"

"Yes, don't ask me why, but—"

"There is no need to explain but at the very least allow me to get you an umbrella."

I would agree to this request because he would only mother me until I did. "Yes, very well."

He rushes off toward the security desk and retrieves what I think is a black golfing umbrella. "I knew it was here somewhere." He mutters to himself as he walks back toward me.

"You're too kind."

"Not at all, and if you should require collecting from wherever it is you are heading, please do not hesitate to call."

"I don't think that will be necessary, Forbes, but I appreciate the offer."

"Not at all, Mr Delaney."

"Call me Dalton, please." I'd been asking him for the better part of two years, and he was still unable to do so. "I'd much prefer it."

Rather than agree to my request, he offers his customary nod. Not wanting to idly chat any longer than necessary I rush out of the huge glass doors and prepare to do battle with Mother Nature.

A strong wind almost knocks me off balance as I look up at the sky. "Wow..." I have no other words for what I'm witnessing but I sense something amiss almost instantly. Stepping into the night air, the world feels off kilter, out of balance even. Was it the rush of heat I wasn't expecting or that strange smell in the air?

I couldn't put my finger on it, but another flash of lightning demands my attention and draws my eyes toward the Albert Dock complex. I'd spent many nights socialising there, so it wasn't an unfamiliar place to me.

Dalton.

I'm positive I hear somebody call my name, but once again, I'm alone. For a moment, I wonder if I'm dreaming but pinching the skin on my hand tells me I'm wide awake.

As I near the gates to the main entrance, lights in bars and restaurants around the dock flicker off, plunging the waterfront into a near darkness aside from the moonlight reflecting off the River Mersey. Turning toward the Arena, its lights now dim too, I realise my home city has never been this quiet.

It's quite a special moment and matched by the eerie silence, I feel I've stepped into a parallel world.

Suddenly, words I've never given much thought to marched front and centre into my mind. I speak them out loud.

"This is a special place for lovers! Interlock your padlocks on to the railings and throw away the key into the Mersey. You will never lose your true love!" Love Locks at the Albert Dock is a special place. Padlocks are secured to chains on the bridge by couples in love. But as it was something I'd never done, why did I feel compelled to go there?

My parents are apprehensive, but the decision has been made.

Deep in the bowels of the palace, my world's biggest open secret sat undisturbed.

"I can't believe the size of this place."

"You must never speak of the gate outside these walls," my father warns. "To do so is punishable by life imprisonment."

"You have my word." Although it's obvious others had been here and probably made the same promise, some had spoken out of turn, but for me, their lack of discretion could only be seen as a blessing.

Mother is hovering on the side-lines. Her gaze is set on what is meant to remain unspeakable, but I'm certain I'm not the only one here that can hear whispers in the distance. We cannot see what lies in the darkness, or beyond it, but there is something there. "You know what to do when you are ready to return."

I nod, eager to be on my way. "I do."

"Press the locator and we will see the signal and open the gate to bring you back."

"Thank you, Father."

"Remember your promise," he reminds me.

"Of course." I embrace each of them in turn. "I'm ready to go."

"We don't know what awaits you or how the journey will affect you but close your eyes and step through, but beware, when you reach your destination, you may be disorientated, so take a minute to get your bearings."

When rumours of its existence were first whispered to me at a political social gathering I'd been forced to attend, I imagined some huge bright and shiny science fiction style object. In reality, it is anything but. Only a simple metal walkway that leads to a dark tunnel stands before me. I suspect in the darkness, the terrifying unknown, is where I will cross the divide from my universe to his. "Where will I end up?"

"Exactly where you are now, but the palace will not exist on the other side." At times, I sensed he knew more than he was prepared to reveal. For now, he seems sure of himself and his ability to retrieve me should I deviate from the plan. Had he too crossed the bridge in secret, and if so, why?

"How am I supposed to find him?"

"That is entirely up to you, Raven," Mother advises. Her tone is one of uncertainty of my mission succeeding. "You are the only person we know of that has made this perilous journey, but I suggest you use the technology available to you there."

"I guess so..."

"Whatever you do, you must not place yourself in danger, do you hear me?" It is the first time I'd ever seen fear in my father.

"Understood."

"Come back to us safe and sound, do you hear me, Raven?"

"I will, I swear."

"Twenty-four hours and if you haven't returned, I will come through the gate to find you."

"That won't be necessary, Father. I know what I must do."

"We love you, Raven." Mother wiped away her tears with the back of a gloved hand.

"I love you both."

Without another word, I hold onto the sides of the walkway and head toward the darkness. Almost forgetting, I shove my hand into the pocket of my jeans. *Thank God!* For a moment I worry I've forgotten to pick up the solid silver engraved padlock the jeweller had engraved for me only yesterday. I intend to leave a piece of me behind and could think of no better tribute. Looking down at the precious object, I read the inscription,

My World.
My Heart.
My Love.
My Life.
Now & Forever More... Raven x

They are words that capture my feelings perfectly.

Pushing it back into my pocket, I'm finally ready. Still, fear grips me and holds me in thrall. For a moment I consider turning back until a whooshing noise startles me. I'm forced to relinquish my grip on the metal handrail.

I feel like I've been lassoed and dragged unwillingly into the air. Air is forced out of my lungs and leaves me gasping for breath. Terror strikes because I feel nothing under foot. All thought and reason leaves me.

And then in the blink of an eye my feet find solid ground once more.

I inhale a lungful of air, and then another until the burning in my back subsides.

Bent double, I feel zapped of all energy and fall to my knees, pain ricocheting from my knees upwards. I find my voice. "Oh, my…" Then, I vomit as the world around me begins to spin or at least that's how it feels. Father was correct. I am disorientated, but I remain on my knees, dry retching, willing it to pass. And it does, then a whole other world presents itself to me.

I'm home, or somewhere that closely resembles the place I left behind.

Everything about it, my country's capital city seems familiar. But on second glance I could be on an alien world.

The skyline I recognise, the streets, the bars, every place we'd ever visited together right where they ought to be. But a strange aroma lingers in the air.

Thunder booms above, startling me. I've never heard such cacophony in the atmosphere, as though the universe is telling me I don't belong here.

It would be right—I exist in a place with another who is identical to me, in appearance at least, if not DNA. This world will fight to expel me and put right what is now out of sync with my uninvited presence.

I arrive safe and sound, but the hard part will be finding him.

Looking to the stars magnified brilliantly and brighter than where I come from, I whisper, hoping that somehow, he will hear me, "Thank you, Father."

I recall his stark warning. *One* night only, Raven.

Putting one foot in front of the other, I don't know what I expect. Gravity is the same here. I'm still human and being here gives me no other abilities aside from the fact I'm getting a chance my own universe took from me.

The sound of the river in the distance steals my attention. A quick look around then I would search for an internet café and see what information was available to me.

Will he have the same name? I have no clue what to expect. I'm supposed to be the first from my world to cross the divide, or so I'm meant to believe.

Walking along the waterfront, the Marina sits to my right. It's then I realise my father is correct in his assumption. Where the palace sits in my world, here it is an empty parking lot.

I'm on borrowed time and have to formulate a plan and fast. Use what technology is available to me; that's what mother said, and she was correct. Leaving without seeing him isn't an option so I decide to take a route I'm familiar with in the hope it will help me to succeed with my mission.

I remember the padlock in my pocket and think of Love Locks at the Albert Dock. My eternal tribute had to remain there. Thankfully, I'd had the foresight to commission the padlock in a material that would never rust. I'd left one key on the other side. The one in my pocket will find its resting place at the bottom of the River Mersey.

It's only a five-minute walk from where I stand but in such awful weather and a flimsy coat, I know I'll be drenched before I reach my destination. But I won't leave without locking my words into the world. *A little water won't kill you.* My inner voice scolds my indecision. *Just get on with it!*

Four - Love Locks

Rain falls in sheets, and even with an umbrella and warm wool coat, I'm soaked through to my skin. Strangely though, it's a warm night. Atmospheric is what TV weather people would call it.

I've never seen such a downpour, not since I was caught up in a tropical storm during a trip to Havana, Cuba two years ago. I shake my head when thinking back to that time. Stupidly, I'd agreed to storyboard the visuals for a well-known, multi-million selling singer's promotional video—not my finest hour, but if truth be told, I was wooed by the exorbitant fee.

Picking up the pace, I begin to think leaving the penthouse in this maelstrom was a bad idea. But something urges my feet to move forward, rather than turn back.

I think of Love Locks again,

This is a special place for lovers!
Interlock your padlocks on to the railings and throw away the key into the Mersey.
You will never lose your true love!

"As if," I say too loudly with a half-hearted laugh because I have yet to find a steady girlfriend, never mind a true love.

Yes, I can write about love. I do it daily. Film and television bosses lap it up. Romance sells, but does it reflect true life? Not for me, but I haven't given up on the idea of true love, it just hasn't happened, yet!

I feel at peace as I stroll past the Marina and tell myself I should do it more, that I shouldn't lose myself to the glitz and glamour of the entertainment world. I have more money than I know what to do with but with no significant other to share it with, what am I working so hard for?

I'm almost twenty-eight. I look good and take care of myself. I'm a catch so why am I wandering around a deserted Liverpool en-route to a place where couples in love go to solidify their relationship by leaving a lasting tribute?

Maybe the storm has messed with my head, who knows, but whatever my misgivings I'm here, but still alone.

If my life right now were a scene from one of those God-awful Disney movies, my Princess would be running toward me, arms outstretched with a radiant smile drawn on. The obligatory big ballad would play out in the background. But this isn't a cartoon. It's real life!

"You've lost it, Dalton."

Now I'm talking to myself.

Despite the madness of the unusual situation I find myself in, it's the first time in months I feel connected to who I am. Born and bred in Liverpool, I'd spent far too long away, holed up in hotel and conference rooms storyboarding and re-writing at the behest of idiot directors who couldn't write a shopping list for themselves.

Why can't I have my own happily ever after ending?

I look out toward the river as lightning illuminates the skies. Has the universe just answered me, and if so, what is it trying to tell me?

My mind is awash with thoughts of past, present, and future. Thinking whiles away the time and minutes later I arrive at my destination.

I glance at the river, over to the large town beyond. Its lights twinkling. Strangely enough, that side of the water doesn't seem to be affected by our adverse conditions. An anomaly perhaps, but certainly unusual and the stuff of alien invasion or disaster movies.

I kneel to read the padlocks and feel I am intruding on people's private lives. I can't help thinking; *perhaps there's a story here*?

"What a mess my life is." I speak although nobody is there to hear me.

Why do I feel so pensive, yet reflective?

Take a long look at yourself and tell me what you see. I feel like God has held up a large mirror and forced me to take a long look at who I am and what I want. I don't like the answers to my self-invoked questions. That's my brother's job. He's two years older than I am and is considered the intelligent one in the family; a well-known shrink by day and author by night. He's a celebrity in his own right, smart and articulate, where I'm deemed the creative one. He takes great pleasure in lecturing me, but I usually turn my nose up; blissful, ensconced in a world where my arse was kissed on a daily basis; a vacuous existence I hadn't seen until standing on what seemed to be a precipice.

Change is coming but from which direction and where, I have no idea.

I've been standing in this same position, looking out across the River Mersey, not realising the rain has stopped until footsteps pull me from my innermost thoughts.

I'm not alone.

Wondering who lurks close by, I turn and am pleasantly surprised by the beautiful woman staring back at me.

Are those tears I see running down her cheeks? I don't know for sure because she's soaked too, and shivering.

"Thank God the rain has stopped," is all I can think of to say. Hardly the best conversation starter but it's the best I have on the hop.

Five - Face to Face

Startled, I feel the air sucked out of my lungs. My eyes are locked into his as I fight to draw breath.

Is it really you? The words I am desperate to speak will not come.

"Are you okay?" *His face, his voice, everything as I remember it.* "Are you hurt?" Shaking my head is all I can manage to do but I know that look on his face. Concern creeps in. He's thinking the worst. "Miss, do you understand what I am saying?"

"Yes." I take a deep breath and clear my throat. "Sorry, you startled me is all. I wasn't expecting you, err, I mean anybody to be here so late, or is it early?"

"Can I help you with anything?" He slipped out of his coat. "Here, you're soaking wet and must be freezing."

I felt chilled to my bones. "No, please, there is little point in us both getting wet."

"Nonsense." He approaches cautiously and drapes his wool coat over my shoulders. "I'm sorry, I got a little wet too, but you'll catch your death if not careful."

Catch your death... He used to say that to me. "Thank you, erm..."

"My name is Dalton Delaney, and you are?"

Dalton. Relief covered me like a warm blanket. *My Dalton.*

"I am Raven Delaney..." I quickly corrected my words, admonishing myself for the faux pas. "Sorry, the cold you know... my name is Raven Andre."

"It is my pleasure to meet you, Raven Andre."

"Thank you, but the pleasure is all mine."

He stared at me with curious eyes. "You look familiar. Have we met before?"

Is it possible that his soul recognises mine? "I don't think so. I'm not from around here."

"Really, you sound like you're local."

"My parents are from here and moved to London when I was a baby, but I've always wanted to visit so decided on a last-minute trip."

"Ah, that must be it then." His smile disarms me; perfect straight, white teeth. "Are they with you?"

"Sadly not, they are vacationing on the other side of the err, world."

"That's a shame. You're visiting your birthplace for the first time and they aren't here to show you the wonderful sights this city has to offer."

"*You* could show me around if you wish?" I was behaving in too bold a manner but couldn't help myself. It was the first time since my husband died that I felt settled and at peace inside. The war between head and heart held a temporary ceasefire. "If you have nothing else to do, that is?"

"Now, you mean?"

"If you like?"

"Well, okay, yes, if you're happy to be escorted by a stranger."

"I can tell you're a good man." I fought the urge to wrap my arms around him.

"You can?" He seemed surprised.

"Yes."

"Are you sure we've never met?" He looked deep into my eyes. If only they could tell him what I was forbidden to reveal.

"I don't think I would ever forget meeting such a charming man."

"This isn't some crappy chat-up line but there's something familiar about you."

I was going out on a limb, but it seems I had little control over what came next. "Souls destined to meet, maybe?"

"Do you believe in all that?"

"I believe that two people who are meant to be together will always find a way."

"I've never been lucky in love, and while I might not go in for the whole destiny thing, it's a nice way to look at it."

I had to change the subject, and fast. I didn't trust my own strength to do the right thing. "What is it you do for a living, Dalton?"

"I work in the television and film industry."

"You're an actor?" My Dalton was Vice President, second only to my father. In this matter, they were worlds apart.

"God, no." He laughed. "I'd be bloody awful—no I'm a screenwriter."

"You write movies?"

"Kind of, yes…"

"Wow, I am impressed."

"I love my job, but I've written some absolute howlers in my time."

"I'm afraid I don't watch much television and rarely get a chance to go to the movies."

"If I may, what is it you do?"

"Not much these days."

"Oh?"

"I was a housewife."

"Was?"

"I lost my husband some months back and…"

He took my hands in his and by the look on his face, we both felt the same surge of energy pass between us. "I am so sorry to hear that." He looked down at my hands in his. I sensed his confusion but felt serenity in his touch.

"Thank you. I won't pretend it's been easy, but I'm using this trip in the hope of pushing forward with my life, just as he'd have wanted."

"May I ask how he died?"

Thunder rumbled above us, threatening another downpour. Was it the universe telling me to tread carefully? "He fell whilst rock climbing."

"Jesus Christ, that's awful, Raven."

"I'm not over it, not even close, but he would hate me wallowing in grief."

"There's no time limit on grief, so don't push yourself too hard."

"Sometimes I wish there were, because it wouldn't hurt as much as it does now." I swallowed hard, not wanting him to see my vulnerability.

"How do you ever get over losing the love of your life?"

"You see what he meant to me, don't you?"

"I watch people, Raven which is why I see in your eyes what words cannot. He was and still is everything to you."

I pull the padlock and key from my pocket and stare at the words. "My World. My Heart. My Love. My Life," I recite.

"The perfect inscription—he would love it."

My heart fluttered, but I had to remind myself, it really wasn't my Dalton, just a close copy. "What makes you think so?"

"Because it would mean everything to me, to think somebody loved me that much."

"Wherever he is, I hope he knows how happy he made me."

"True love is written in the stars, Raven, never forget that."

His words shook me. "My mother once said the same thing to me. Do you really believe it?"

"I'd like to think we have a preordained destiny but I'm a sceptic by nature." He paused, as though lost for a moment. "Still, it doesn't stop me wishing and hoping that one day I'll meet the woman of my dreams."

"You're single?"

"Afraid so."

"Why?"

"I've just never met the one."

"That's sad."

"I agree but fate is a funny old thing, and who knows what it has planned for me."

"Maybe meeting a strange woman at Love Locks is your fate?"

"Something drew me out into the night—why shouldn't it be you?"

"That's quite the romantic way to look at it."

"Perhaps it was your destiny to meet me, a stranger, and pour your heart out to him?"

"You must think me crazy."

"I guess I should but I'm wary and captivated by you in equal measure."

"Wary?"

"Yes, but I don't mean to offend."

"Why wary?"

"Because I've only just met you and feel like I've known you all of my life."

I was chancing my luck in the hope something magical might happen. "Perhaps in a parallel universe we're good friends?"

"Wouldn't that be something?"

"Yes, Dalton, it really would."

Soulmates. A word I loathe, but one that bounces around my mind, and has done since Raven walked into my life only minutes ago. "So, what do you have planned for the rest of the, erm, what is it now, the early hours of the morning?"

"Nothing really, I was just out for a walk and got caught in the rain and as luck would have it, I bumped into a kind man who offered me his coat."

"Are you staying close by?"

"My family own property about ten minutes away from here."

"I can walk back that way with you, if you'd like, see you safely home?" Then I realised how my words came across. The cliché of all clichés; the single man wanting a 'coffee' and whatever came afterwards.

"It's fine, really, Dalton, I've taken up far too much of your time already."

"It would be my pleasure, and before you think it, I'm not some arsehole wanting a quick bunk up."

She smiled and her whole face lit up, a true vision. "I don't think that at all, but I'm only in the city for twenty-four hours, and if there is a coffee shop open anywhere, I'd love it if you would escort me there."

"I'd love a coffee right now."

"And maybe cake too."

Could she be any more perfect? "Anything you fancy." I had cupboards stocked with food, cakes, biscuits, the works, and coffee from all around the world, but asking her back to my place might be a step too far.

"Okay, but before we go, I just need to leave this here." She opened her hand and the padlock glinted in the moonlight.

"I'll give you a moment alone."

"No, it's fine, I'd like it if you'd stay."

"I don't want to intrude."

"You're not." Instead, I take a few steps back as she kneels on the cold hard ground. With the key, she pops the lock and in a moment that touches me immeasurably, kisses it, then fastens it around the chain with so many others. Then without word she throws the key into the water. "My love will always be yours…" I feel I've intruded on a special moment, but inner thoughts tells me I would not want to be anywhere else. In quiet reflection, she stands and looks out across the river. Then she turns to me and speaks in a tone immersed in heartbreak. "I'm ready to go now."

"Are you sure?"

"Positive." We fell into step together while my mind raced to think of a coffee shop open all hours. Would any actually be open now?

As though she had read my mind, she spoke. "Perhaps the bad weather means we won't find anywhere still open?"

"I'm not sure, but I have a suggestion but feel free to say no."

"Okay."

"I live close by. You're more than welcome to come back to mine and dry off. Then if you're hungry. I can find you a bite to eat?"

"Don't you have to get some sleep?"

"I have nothing planned–only a meeting with my accountants, which was cancelled late last night," I lie. "My building is serviced and there is a 24 hour Concierge on duty, so you'll be perfectly safe with me."

"You don't have to explain anything to me, Dalton, I trust you."

"I'm glad you do, but not everyone is decent."

"You are, I know it."

"Shall we go?"

"I'm quite famished, so yes, let's go."

Ten minutes later, we step into the foyer of my building.

Forbes rushes to greet us. He nods his greeting to Raven then addresses me. "Mr Delaney, you should have called me."

"I wasn't far away."

"Come, let me call the elevator and get you both settled into a warm room."

"Forbes, this is my friend, Raven."

"It is a pleasure to meet you, Forbes." She held out her hand.

He took it. "The pleasure is all mine, Miss Raven."

With his hand placed on her elbow, he guided her to the elevator and pressed the call button. "Can I get either of you anything?"

"No thank you, Forbes. Have a good evening."

"You too, Sir." He nodded then turned to Raven. "I do hope we meet again, Miss."

She smiled then leaned in to kiss his cheek. "Thank you."

He seems touched by her gesture and held a hand to his cheek. The elevator doors opened. "Goodnight to you both."

The doors closes. "What a lovely man."

"He's a good guy and takes care of me."

Thirty seconds later the doors open into a spacious open plan living room. "You must be pretty successful to live here."

"I do ok, but it's a bit big for just me." I took her hand. "Come this way." I walk her toward the open fireplace. With the touch of a button, flames offer instant warmth.

"How lovely."

I point to the rug. "Here, sit in front of the fire and I'll go brew the coffee and see what goodies I have."

"Lovely."

I rushed toward the bedroom and grabbed the clean towelling robe hanging behind the door. Heading back to her, she was on her feet. "Would you mind if I used your bathroom?"

"Of course not, and look, I got this for you to wear. Feel free to jump in the shower, this should keep you warm and I can put your clothes in the dryer."

"You're too kind."

"It's entirely up to you, no pressure."

"I will shower if you don't mind."

"My home is yours. The guest bathroom is on the next floor. Just leave your clothes outside the door and I'll pop up and put them in the dryer."

"Thank you, Dalton."

I watch as she makes her way to the next floor then dive into the kitchen to put fresh coffee on. Opening the larder cupboard, I send a silent thank you to the universe as the delicious aroma hits me. My wonderful housekeeper has been to my favourite bakery–freshly baked scones and lemon drizzle cake make my mouth water. Pulling them out of the cupboard, I set them on my best dishes then place it on the coffee table with napkins, nearest to the fire.

Then I dash up the stairs, retrieve her wet clothes and shove them in the tumble dryer which is perfectly located in the laundry room next door. I slip out of my wet clothes and dump them in the washing basket. Finding clean jeans and a T-shirt, I towel dry my hair and I'm done. My eyes are irritated, so I remove the lenses and put my tortoiseshell glasses on.

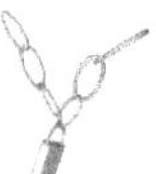

Fifteen minutes later, my eyes follow her shapely legs as she walks carefully down the stairs wearing my fluffy towelling robe. Without a scrap of make-up, she is still the most beautiful woman I've ever seen. Her blonde hair is now dry and straight; she found the hairbrush in the cabinet.

"Did you find everything you need?"

"I feel much better, thank you."

"Are you warm enough?"

"I'm toasty, but if you don't mind, I'll sit in front of the fire for a few minutes."

"Of course, but please excuse me while I fetch the coffee. Help yourself to whatever you want from the plate."

"Wow, you're simply amazing."

"Not me I'm afraid...it's my housekeeper you need to thank." I rush into the kitchen.

Seven - Flames of Desire

I feel comfortable in his presence. He isn't my Dalton, but I like him, and even though being in his presence forces my emotions to the surface, I already dread the moment I'll have to say goodbye to him. But I cannot exist here, not without potentially warping reality. The consequences to both worlds could be severe, and I won't risk that.

Plus, I'd promised my parents I'd return, and as much as my heart screams at me to take the risk and stay, I can't hurt them.

Say goodbye, I tell myself. *Then find a way to live again.*

He returns from the kitchen carrying a tray with a coffee pot and two large mugs. "Sorry for the delay."

"Don't be silly, you are the perfect host." I'm not sure if the flush to my cheeks is caused by the fire or him being in such close proximity. After all, under this robe, I am naked. "Oh, I just noticed your glasses, how distinguished you look."

"I usually wear lenses unless I'm at home."

"They suit you." Another difference to my Dalton. He had perfect 20/20 vision.

"I'm glad you think so." He sits next to me on the expensive-looking rug. "Shall I pour?"

"Yes, and I'll get the plate of goodies." I climb to my knees then onto my feet, grab the plate and find my spot again.

"I brought out a selection of everything so tuck in, don't be shy."

"You'll find where cake and pastries are concerned, I have no shame."

"You're my kind of girl," he replies, a flush rising to his cheek. "Erm, are you warm enough?"

"Everything is simply perfect." It's not because I'll leave him soon. We'll never see one another again. He hands me a cup filled with black coffee. I inhale the delicious aroma. Strong and black, just how I like it.

"Sorry, I didn't think. Would you like milk and sugar?"

"It's good the way it is."

"You can tell I don't have many guests."

"Nonsense, you're an absolute gentleman, Dalton, and any woman would be lucky to claim you as her own."

He takes a sip of his coffee then sets it down on the fireplace. I follow suit, my appetite suddenly vanishing.

The lights flicker a few times then we are cast into darkness with only the flames of the fire providing an orange glow.

"Oh, shit, I'm sorry." He made to jump to his feet, but I rest my hand on his, wanting him to stay.

"Don't be—I like it."

Rain hammers against the windows; the storm has worked itself up again, this time into a frenzy. Rumbles of thunder followed by lightning heighten the pent-up atmosphere in the room.

"I think the gods are angry."

I am suddenly filled with dread. Is it my presence here that has caused such awful conditions? "Somebody must have really annoyed them."

He shrugs and I catch his look in his eyes as the flames of the fire flicker. "We're in here, safe and warm, who cares what they do?"

"I have to leave at some point, come rain or shine."

"Not if you don't want to."

"I don't want to..." The truth seeps out. "...but I must."

"Perhaps one day soon, you can come back?"

"There's nothing I'd love more." It's an outright lie, but what else can I say?

"Me too." He leans closer toward me. And then I feel it, that moment between us; one I should fight with everything I have, but one I don't have the strength or desire to.

Our lips meet. It is destiny that pushes us together rather than wanting to tear us apart.

I close my eyes, surrendering to the moment.

The robe slips, exposing my bare shoulder. His fingers make contact, sending a rush of energy through me.

Too lost in his kiss to care, being with him feels natural, familiar, easy. Lost in his arms, I experience a sense of tranquillity, that everything wrong in my life had righted itself. Of course, I'm cheating fate by stepping into this new world, but it won't last forever, how could it? A quick battle rages in my mind but soon resolves itself as I lie on the rug, pulling Dalton toward me. "Make love to me, please."

"Are you sure that's what you want?"

"I need you." All of my sadness and insecurities are suddenly visible. He cannot fail to see them.

"I want to, but you're still grieving—"

I cut in quickly. "Only you can help me." It's the truth, and while my heart wants to tell him everything, he'll never believe me. I crush my lips against his, taking a handful of his hair, ensuring he can't pull back from me.

He pushes his chiselled body against mine. Then I slip completely out of the robe, my naked body illuminated by flame light. Pulling the T-shirt over his head, I marvel at his body, then I throw it across the room. My fingers expertly unfasten his button. He wriggles out of the jeans and kicks them away.

"You are truly the most amazing woman I've ever met."

I smile, then pull him on top of me. His hard cock is pressed against me and flashes of my Dalton warn me not to confuse them both. "I want to feel you inside me."

"I don't have condoms."

"It's ok, I trust you."

As he pushes his cock inside me. I gasp then feel a surge of adrenalin.

Our bodies move in perfect harmony, each of us taking cues from the other. He makes the perfect lover. A streak of jealousy runs through me because he can never be mine, but thanks to him, I get my wish. I know I want more but a promise is a promise.

Eight - Dance With Me

We made love for what seemed like hours. I've never experienced anything like it. Kismet was something that belonged in the movies but now I wasn't so sure.

She looks into my eyes and I can see her longing for somebody to love. "Come with me."

"Where?" She draws me onto the balcony, out into the pouring rain. "You'll get sick being out here with no clothes on."

She shrugs her shoulders, her carefree attitude refreshing. "I don't care, dance with me."

"What, dance with you here, now, in the rain?"

"Where better than the here and now?"

I catch the subtle meaning behind her words. Fate has been a cruel mistress and robbed her of the man she loved. All she has left are her memories of him and the here and now. "I'm not a very good dancer. Raven, and there's no music."

"That doesn't matter, just wrap your arms around me and move."

I can't find it in myself to refuse her and do as she asks. "How's that?"

"Wonderful."

In seconds, our naked bodies glisten with rain. It doesn't seem to matter to either of us. We sway under biting rain and swirling thunderclouds, but there is nowhere else I'd rather be.

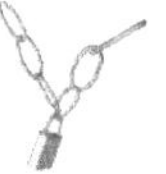

I don't know how long we remained outside for last night, but I wake as she kisses my lips and the warm sun peeps over the horizon.

"Good morning."

I notice she is already dressed. "Did you sleep well?"

"Like a baby."

"Can I make you some breakfast?"

"I really should leave. I've taken up far too much of your time already."

"Do you have to go?"

"I don't want to, but…"

"Then stay," I interrupt, "even for a little while."

"I can't."

"You can do anything you want."

"I don't belong here, Dalton."

"Of course you do, you were born here, remember."

"You don't understand."

"Then help me to."

"This isn't my world."

"I know, but London is only a few hours away, what's the rush to get back there."

"I'm afraid if I don't go now, I never will."

"Last night, you know when I said I felt like I've known you forever…?"

"Yes of course."

"I meant it, every word."

She held my face in her hands. "You're the sweetest man, but I can't stay."

"Tell me why?"

"I made a promise."

"To whom?"

"My parents." I'm more confused than ever. "You see, after losing my husband, I felt stifled, suffocated, lost in my grief, so I decided to get away, and come here, and it's helped more than you'll ever realise."

"That's a good thing, right?"

"Yes, it is but my parents didn't want me to come."

"I'll take care of you."

"I don't doubt you would but staying here would cause all kinds of complications."

"For whom?"

"All of us,"

"You're talking in riddles, Raven."

"I wish I could tell you everything, but my father is very powerful. If I don't go, he will come for me."

I couldn't fathom any parents treating their own child so badly they would stand in the way of what could be her happiness. "I don't know what to say."

"We can't uproot our lives for one night."

"It meant more to me than that."

"I'm sorry, Dalton."

"And I know we only just met, but it meant something to you too."

"It meant the world to me, but not enough for me to stay." She climbed to her feet and brushed herself down.

I looked up into her eyes. "Don't go, please."

"I have to, but I want you to promise me one thing. Will you?"

I felt my heart thudding in my chest. "If I can."

"Meet a good woman and be happy."

"I met her, last night."

"I'm not the one for you."

"You don't know that."

"I do."

"How?"

"Because I already met the one and lost him."

Her words hit me like a juggernaut. I'm angry but have no words with which to reply nor would I wish to be cruel. She used me, it happens, but what eats away at me; I failed to see it. Did I believe in love at first sight before meeting her? No, I didn't, but I do now. I've fallen in love with the mysterious Raven. But are my feelings one-sided? I feel such a fool. "Then you're right, you should go."

"Before I leave, and I know I have no right, but would you do something for me?"

"What?"

She pulls me to my feet.

"I want to look into your eyes and say goodbye to you properly."

"You don't have to do this—"

She silences me with a kiss. I close my eyes for a moment and feel I'm under a magical spell. I savour the moment. Then I sense she is done and open my eyes.

Her gaze is locked into mine.

Seeing tears fall down her cheeks affects me more than I want to admit to.

"Goodbye, Dalton." She kisses my cheek then turns away.

I am forced to watch as this magnificent creature walks out of my life.

Nine - The Gift

The months passed by in a flurry of activity.

I'd passed between worlds, but ultimately and against my own wishes, I kept my promise and returned to where I belonged.

As much as my heart ached and continues to do so, I'd made the right decision, if not for me, but others.

I finally found the strength to let go of my Dalton. But he is never far away from my thoughts. Day after day I pray for his forgiveness; I'd sought comfort in the arms of another for reasons I hope he would understand.

Now, my reasons for existing are not motivated by self, but for the needs of another.

I rock my baby boy, Noah, gently in my arms and think more about the blessings than what I have lost. He is my world and my reason for being.

I cannot lose myself to the horrors of the past because there is another who depends entirely on me. He is only two days old yet from the moment I set eyes upon him, I would sacrifice everything for his happiness.

Dalton. I cast my mind back nine months and smile. Just one night and I was given the most precious gift of all, a child of my own. But our laws are absolute, and Noah will never know his father. For that reason, I will always feel guilt, but I resolved to tell him the whole truth, when he is old enough to understand.

"Good morning, darling." Mum sweeps into the room. Already she is the doting grandmother. "And how is that divine little man today?"

"Hungry."

"You were just the same, latching on whenever you could."

"Ugh, too much information."

"Don't be silly, Raven."

"Where's Father?"

"In a meeting at the Houses of Parliament."

"Oh, I wasn't aware he had anything planned."

"I'm not supposed to say anything but over the last few months he has been in discussions with ministers about The Gate."

Why had I not been kept in the loop? "Why?"

"Apparently, there have been crossings over the last hundred years, many more than we were led to believe."

"I thought I was the first."

"Yes, and I was the first woman on Mars, darling—it's not supposed to be common knowledge."

"So, what is being proposed; shutting it down?"

"Quite the opposite actually."

"What aren't you saying, Mother?"

"Your father has successfully lobbied the ministers to allow crossings for what he deems research purposes."

"Wow." I held Noah close to me. "And what will that entail?"

"Well—"

We were interrupted by my father's untimely arrival. "How are you today, Raven?"

"Tired but fine."

"And Noah?"

"Hungry."

"Aren't they all at that age."

He sits beside me and gazes adoringly at his grandson. "Would you like to hold him?"

"Not right now."

"Why ever not?" I have asked him repeatedly. Is he afraid to hold a new-born?

"It doesn't seem right."

"Phillipe, please."

"Before you jump to conclusions, Adriana, please hear me out."

"Can we not do this in front of the baby?"

"The reason I have not yet held that precious boy is simple."

Mother huffed. Her impatience is evident. "And are you going to let us into this mystery, or do we need to start a guessing game?"

"The child should be held by his father before anybody else."

Sadness overwhelms me. "I wish that could be, but we know differently."

"I recall saying to you not so long ago that you are my world and that your mother and I were blessed with your birth and that I would do what I could to ensure your happiness."

"Yes, I remember but what of it?"

"Having you brought untold joy into our lives, and whatever our achievements, you are the greatest of them all."

My hormones are still out of whack and tears fall easily. "Aww, Daddy, you're making me cry." Even Mother dabs at her eyes.

"So, with that being said, and with the full backing of my government, you are to be our special envoy and the only one authorised to journey through the gate until we are assured it is safe to do so. Then and only then will longer expeditions take place."

Both mother and I gasp.

"Are you joking?"

"Why would I joke about such a serious matter?"

"So, I can cross, and it doesn't have to be a secret?"

"The existence of The Gate must remain confidential."

"Oh, Phillipe, the people already suspect."

"Yes, Adriana, but I will confirm it's official existence only when the time is right."

Adrenaline pumped through my veins. "I can take Noah to see his daddy."

"There are far more qualified to undertake this assignment, but you are trusted because you are our daughter."

Mother threw her arms around my father and smothered his cheek in kisses. "You sentimental old fool."

I'm too stunned to speak.

"It is purely a political decision, Adriana, and nothing more."

"Oh, hush, Phillipe, we both know why you did it."

"I don't know what to say."

"The boy deserves to know his father and you deserve to be happy." He pauses for a moment, always one to choose his words wisely. "and if you can find that happiness existing between both worlds, you have my blessing and that of our government."

"So, they know who Noah's father is?"

"I told them the truth, well a version of it."

"What version would that be?" Mother enquired.

"That I sent you Raven on a secret mission to ascertain facts about our doppelgangers and well, nature took its course."

"How did they take it?" I knew from experience most in government like things to remain just so.

"Some were not happy, but what's done is done."

"Are you in danger of losing your job?" I would hate my actions to be the reason he is denied the chance to lead the country he loves.

"Not at all." His sideways glance at my mother tells me otherwise. "Just don't make me regret my part in it."

"I promise, you won't regret it, nor will those old dinosaurs."

"You have two weeks until your first mission so there is much to discuss."

"Can I take Noah with me?"

"You can, but your mother has special dispensation, if she should so wish, to travel with you, until you're back to full strength that is."

"I can't believe this...here, Mother, take Noah." She took him from me. He stirred a little but soon settled. I was still a little sore from the birth, but with a little effort I found my feet and threw my arms around my father. "I love you so much, thank you."

"Your happiness matters more to me than any job, remember that."

I close my laptop, too weary to continue working.

Having spent the last ten months dreaming of her, I hadn't had a decent night's sleep since.

Seeing her face; remembering her touch, us holding one another as we danced cheek to cheek through the worst storm in recorded history. Those moments would stay with me forever. For one night, I felt true love.

Now, I did everything I could to convinced myself I'd dreamt it. It hurt less that way. But no matter how I tried to fool myself, Raven existed. I know because I've watched the building's CCTV recordings time and again.

I've tried to find her many times and spent a fortune doing so. It's like she dropped off the face of the planet.

But I have little to go on. All I know is what she told me. She could have conjured a make believe name from thin air.

Where is she? I have no answers.

Initially I felt lost, like I'd lost half of me, so I buried myself under a mountain of work, rarely leaving the Penthouse aside from business meetings.

Meeting Raven led to my biggest ever success.

Self-imposed lockdown brought out the creative side of me I'd long considered dead. I sold the rights to my debut novel, Raven's Ghost and to the biggest publishing house in the world, setting a record for the largest advance offered to an author. Then, Paramount Studios bought the film rights and fast-tracked production of the movie.

It has been quite the whirlwind for a number of reasons and though one foot is still wedged in the past, in six months, the movie's star-studded world premiere will take place at Grauman's Chinese Theatre in Los Angeles—it's projected to outperform Avatar at the box office.

I've stepped into a world of publicists and photo shoots, and while I'm happy people love my work, my rising success feels hollow because the woman who inspired me to write the book vanished without trace.

Last seen at an empty car park not too far from Love Locks, it seemed she was there one minute and gone the next. Just like a ghost. I went back to where we met just to see if her padlock would yield any clues.

It didn't but seeing the inscription for myself, I understood her a little more.

My World.
My Heart.
My Love.
My Life.
Now & Forever More... Raven x

If she had stayed, I would have been competing with the ghost of her dead husband.

I can't hate her for using me or leaving. In fact, her absence only serves to intensify my feelings for her.

All I want was is one chance to see her again, to thank her if nothing else.

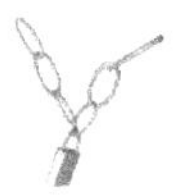

Familiarity is said to breed contempt, but I'm less nervous the second time around.

Instead, Mother stands trembling next to me while my clearly nervous father watches from a safe distance. "Are you ready?" he asks.

Mother nods and keeps a tight hold of my hand.

"It's a go." I give father the thumbs up then wrap my arms protectively around the little boy who sleeps strapped against my chest.

This time my eyes remain wide open as we walk into the darkness.

As fast as a bolt of lightning, we emerge into the light.

It takes a few seconds for my eyes to acclimatise to the daylight.

Looking down, Noah still sleeps soundly, his head against my beating heart. My perfect little boy—even crossing worlds doesn't wake him from slumber. I quickly turn to my mother. "Are you okay?"

The retching sound she makes tells me otherwise. This time the journey had less of an effect, but I pass her the small bottle of water from my pocket.

After a few gulps, she swills her mouth then stands tall. "Right, where to now?"

I point towards Dalton's building. "That way."

I glance at my Rolex watch and groan. "Oh, no!"

01:03pm. I've only slept for an hour but feel exhausted because my sleep pattern is still out of whack. Something familiar about the time pricks my consciousness, but I can't think why.

Slowly losing patience with myself, I roll off the sofa and spring to my feet as the intercom buzzes, aggravating my earlier headache somewhat.

It must be important because I'd asked the day Concierge, Henry, not to bother me otherwise.

"What is it?"

"I am sorry to disturb you, Mr Delaney, but I have a message for you."

"From whom?"

"A Mrs Andre left a note at the desk for your attention."

"I haven't a clue who that is, throw it in the bin and try not to disturb me again."

"You might want to re-think that directive, Sir."

"I beg your pardon."

"Forgive me for speaking out of turn, but the young lady you have been searching for…"

"What about her?" My worsening moods refuses to allow for civility.

"I do believe the young lady is the one who left the note."

"She was there?"

"In reception, yes."

My heart hammers in my chest. Could it be? I don't dare raise my hopes. "What does the note say?"

"One moment please…" I can hear him tearing paper.

"Henry, hurry please."

"It says, Love Locks at the Albert Dock."

"Oh, my God, call me a car, and get it here as fast as you can."

"Five minutes, Sir, it shall be waiting."

I race out of the private elevator and rush toward Henry almost slipping on the freshly buffed marble floor. "Your car is here, and I believe this is yours."

I snatch the letter as I race past then call back to him. "Thank you."

"My pleasure," he shouts after me.

The driver holds the door open for me as I all but throw myself onto the back seat. "Love Locks and fast." It's only minutes away. He slides into the driver's seat and adjusts his hat. "Go! Go! Go!" I order, as he pulls away.

Soulmates. I hear it again, that word. I haven't thought of it since the day she left. But I hear it clear as a ringing bell.

"Sorry about this, Mr Delaney."

Luck isn't on my side. Roadworks block us from moving faster as fear teases, whispering I'll be too late. "I'll get out here."

"Are you sure, we shouldn't be much longer?"

"Yes!" I push the door open. "Sorry, gotta go."

"Past the Arena is the fastest way to get there, Sir."

Dashing off, I forget my manners, but resolve to send a handsome tip later.

My only need is to get there before she believes I'm not coming.

The wind picks up sending shivers coursing through me. I hear its whisper. *Dalton.*

Seconds are the only thing that stand between Raven and me.

I race around the corner and stop dead in my tracks.

Her back is to me, but she isn't alone. There is another, one so similar it must be her mother.

Suddenly I am paralysed and cannot move an inch.

Wind whips at her, forcing her to turn.

Her eyes are wide. Then I see the smile I have never been able to forget. "You came."

Her companion turns. Fighting back tears she places her hand across her mouth.

"Raven, is it really you?"

"Yes, it's me."

"I'm sorry but I can't seem to get my feet to move." She walks toward me as her companion stays put. It's only then I notice the sleeping baby in a pale blue knitted outfit strapped to her. He was covered by her shawl, only revealed by a gust of wind.

"You have a child?"

"I do."

"Is he yours?"

With a nod she confirms the answer to my question. "Dalton, meet Noah, our son."

I fight to remain standing. "Our son?"

"Yes!"

"I-I, don't understand." My brain struggles to process what is obvious. He looks like me. Nearly ten months ago we spent a blissful night together. Still, I ask the question. "How?"

With a warm smile, she spoke. "You'll never believe it when I tell you."

Eleven - Noah's Eyes

Nearly ten months have passed since Raven disappeared from my life, and now she's standing right here, in front of me. I have a yearning to know her secrets, even if she thinks I'll never believe her.

"Try me." I realise I sound harsher than I want to, but she appears back in my life like a ghost from the past, and I'm supposed to just accept it.

Immediately, her eyes convey inner turmoil. She steps away from me, back to the comfort of her companion and the baby in her arms. "If you give me chance to explain, I'll tell you everything you need to know."

I don't want her to be afraid of me and step closer. "I would never harm you, Raven." Then, I look into Noah's eyes, now wide open, and immediately I see myself in them. Any barriers built up to guard my heart come tumbling down. "He really is ours?"

"I'm so sorry, I wanted to return sooner, but–

Her companion finally speaks. "Raven, you must not speak of such things in public."

"I don't think we've been formally introduced." I hold out my hand to greet the stranger, but she's holding the baby. "My name is Dalton Delaney, and you are?"

Her eyes still glisten with tears. "It is wonderful to meet you finally, Mr Delaney–"

"Call me Dalton, please."

"Very well, and you may call me Adriana."

With a nod I acknowledge her. The lofty demeanour and the way she carries herself, chin up and head held high, is almost regal. She hasn't told me yet, but there is little doubt Raven is her daughter. The resemblance between the two is astonishing. "It is my pleasure to meet you too."

"Thank you."

But we have diverted from the crux of the matter.

Where has Raven been for the past ten months and why did she keep her pregnancy and the existence of our child a secret? Why has she returned now? I have many questions that must be answered. But they can wait a little while longer.

I turn my attention to the little man in his grandmother's arms. "And it is the absolute privilege of a lifetime to meet you, Noah." I reach out as Adriana hands him to me. Once settled in my arms, I cradle him close to my chest. Suddenly I feel like I've been hit by an unseen cosmic force, establishing that father/son bond instantly. Blood doesn't lie, it can't, and only delivers ultimate truths. Silent tears fall down Raven's cheeks and I struggle to maintain my own composure. "I'm your Daddy, and I'm going to love you forever and ever."

"I'm sorry I stayed away so long, but there are things I need to tell you that–"

Adriana cuts in once more. "Raven, not here."

I wonder what is so important it cannot be discussed out in the open. "I don't live far away, so why don't we all head back there? Then, we can settle Noah, have a drink and get whatever this is out of the way."

"That sounds wonderful, Dalton." Adriana dabs at her eyes. She is emotional too but aside from introducing her grandson to his father, I can't see the reason for her reaction. Still there is much more to this visit than declaring me a father.

Raven's voice is timid, quiet, as though she is unsure of everything around her. "I don't want you to hate me."

"I've spent the last ten months dreaming about you, I could never hate you."

"Then let us go back to your place and I can finally tell you what I want you to know."

"Would you like to walk, or shall I call a car?"

"I think a car would be better," Raven responds. "Noah is due a feed soon and can get a little tetchy if kept waiting."

"He's got a good appetite, just like his daddy." I look into his wide eyes and the love I feel for him already is like nothing I've ever experienced before.

I call the concierge of my building and ask him to send a car immediately. It's there within five minutes but I say little, so transfixed am I by the little boy in my arms.

Nothing is said on the way back to the penthouse which leaves the atmosphere thick with tension. Noah picks up on it and is unsettled until he latches onto his mother's breast and feeds ferociously. Every move he makes fascinates me—I'm seeing life through a father's eyes while a feeling of love I've never experienced for another swells within me. I know I would give my own life to protect him.

Once fed, and satisfied, Raven settles Noah on the comfy sofa furthest away from the window while I draw the blinds to keep out the worst of the sun.

He's still a little niggly and I'm worried. "Is he okay?"

Adriana answers while Raven tries to settle him. "New surroundings is all, Dalton. Most babies are the same."

"Go to sleep, my darling," Raven coos, brushing her finger gently across his cheek. This seems to settle him. I gaze adoringly at him, still trying to comprehend that an hour ago, I was lost to the past, and now the woman I have spent a fortune trying to find is here with me, and with her, my son.

Adriana walks about the room and appears impressed. "You have done very well for yourself, Dalton."

"Thank you, but your daughter should take some credit for it."

"I should?"

"You are the inspiration for my biggest success."

She appears confused.

"Oh, really?" Adriana comments.

"Yes, really." I point at the enlarged image of the book cover that takes pride of place on the wall above the fireplace. "Have a look for yourself."

"Raven's Ghost, how interesting," Adriana muses. I can't tell how she feels about it.

"You wrote a book, about me?"

"Kind of, yes."

"I don't know what to say."

"I have a copy somewhere, if you'd like to read it."

"That would be lovely," Adriana replies, although the offer was to Raven. Still, it isn't a big deal, but now I see the glint of controlled rage flash in Adriana's eyes. I have displeased her, and though I don't know her, I realise it isn't the best situation to be in.

"Can I get you both a drink?"

"I think you and Raven should talk because it isn't going to get any easier the longer she leaves it." The suggestion is for her daughter, not me. But it makes me anxious. What is it I don't know?

"You're right." She sits on the same sofa Noah dozes on, while I sit opposite. Adriana hovers in the background. "But you'll never believe it when I tell you."

"You already said that, so why don't you let me be the judge."

"Okay, well I should start at the beginning."

"There's no better place, darling." Adriana's rage has subsided and is replaced by concern for her daughter and grandson.

"Well..." Raven says, her voice shaky and unsure. "...our meeting wasn't an accident, in fact, it was carefully planned."

I've never felt so scared, but Dalton deserves to hear the whole truth. And that is, I did engineer our meeting for my own selfish reasons. Little did I know from that meeting I would be blessed with a child to love.

I can't read his expression. While he looks like my Dalton, he has his own personality. I've never seen this reaction. But I aim to remain calm and to answer every question he has. "This is a joke, right?"

"I wouldn't lie about something like this."

He shakes his head, trying to digest what I've just revealed to him. "I'm a screenwriter and successful author; the world of fantastical isn't new to me or beyond any idea of comprehension I might have. But this is like something out of a Hollywood movie."

"It's the truth, Dalton, I swear it on my life and that of our son."

"Do you seriously expect me to believe you've crossed over from some sort of multi-verse to meet me, your dead husband's doppelganger?"

"Every word is true."

"Bullshit," he snaps. "How stupid do you think I am?"

Mother charges across the room as my tears fall. It's not how I want this to be, but I'm naïve to believe he would react any differently. After all, The Gate, or talk of it, doesn't exist on this side. "Choose your words carefully, Mr Delaney," she warns. "I will not tolerate your disrespect of my daughter and all she has suffered to get to where she is now."

He stands up, unafraid of her. The atmosphere between him and my parent is fraught with tension. They stand toe to toe, neither one willing to back down. All the while, Noah kicks his legs and stirs but doesn't wake. "You're happily going along with this madness it seems."

Her eyes darken and her full lips disappear into a thin line of anger. I think of a cobra planning its strike and wonder when she will make her move. Then, with her usual commanding authority, she speaks. "One more word from you, young man, and I will personally throw you over the balcony."

"Mother, please," I protest, looking at my sleeping child. "I don't want any of this."

"Then Mr Delaney should find his manners fast and listen to what you have to say."

"Or what?" Dalton asks. With a shove from her, he falls backwards onto the sofa. "What the...?" His eyes are wide, but he is not the type to strike back against a female, I know that much of him.

She leans over him, and speaks, her tone almost a snarl. "Push my buttons, I dare you."

"I'm not going to be silenced in my own home."

What I dreaded has come to pass. Dalton thinks I'm some sort of fantasist, but how could I have expected him to think anything else.

Mother moves back and Dalton sits up straight. "You do not have to remain silent, but be respectful, and that is all I ask. What my daughter suffered after losing her husband was almost too hard for any parent to bear, but look at your own child sleeping, and tell me you wouldn't move heaven and earth to bring him peace?"

"I would do anything for him, but indulge him in some crazy plot to, well, I don't know what this is all about, but I only believe what I can see with my two eyes, and a parallel world is–"

She holds a finger up to silence him while at the same time retrieves something from her pocket. "Mother, what is that?" I ask.

"My phone."

"I'm not ready to leave yet."

"We are not leaving, Raven, but there are things on this telephone I can show that might make him realise this isn't some sort of elaborate hoax."

"Unless you take me to this other place, nothing you can show me will convince me of its existence."

"Think before you speak, Mr Delaney." She thrusts the telephone into his face. "Watch, and then judge."

"Mother, what are you showing him?"

"Something so spectacular it can't possibly be a sham."

"I am not interested," Dalton protests.

"If you're so sure we are lying, press play, then, if you still think that is the case, we shall leave and never bother you again."

He looked straight at Noah, knowing a relationship with his son is in jeopardy. "Please, Dalton, whatever it is, please watch it."

"I'm only doing it for him, not either of you."

"Whatever," Mother replied, bored of him. "Play the video."

He hits play and holds the phone in both hands. I hear the roar of the crowds on the video and instantly know it is Father's inauguration that he is watching. Mother and I stood proudly alongside him as he was sworn in as President. But there by my side at this solemn and celebratory occasion was my Dalton.

His eyes never left the screen. "What the hell is this?" He finally speaks and I know he's caught a glimpse of his doppelganger.

"That is my Dalton."

"How is this possible?"

"Nothing my daughter told you is a lie, far from it."

Then my heart aches as I hear the voice of the love I lost. "He looks just like me."

Even now, I see no difference in both—I still have to remind myself that my Dalton is gone and the one before me now is somebody entirely new and identical at the same time.

"I came back because you deserve the truth."

"We even sound the same."

"He was a good man," Mother says. "The best in fact, and when we lost him, it left a gaping hole in our family that will never be filled, and no matter where you sit in our future, there is no confusion as to who you are. But at the same time, Raven never had chance to say goodbye, and as time passed by, she lost herself further in grief and misery."

"So, she came here to..."

"To look into your eyes and find some closure, even though you are not him."

I can't speak because emotions bind me and force me back to a time still raw inside. What I wouldn't give for life to be different, but with that is a conundrum because I had to lose my Dalton to have Noah. As much as my heart reaches for what it lost, there is somebody else with needs greater than mine. "I loved him so very much and lost him. I thought coming here would ease my pain, but I returned to my own world and felt I'd lost you too—then I discovered I was pregnant, and while happy you existed here, we existed there." I realise I'm not speaking as succinctly as I can, but this isn't a part in a play rehearsed, it's my life. "What good is any of it if you're not there?"

"Would you have returned if not for Noah?"

"I don't know, but I couldn't get you out of my head, and not as a replacement for what I lost. I believe two souls find one another, and minutes after leaving and returning to my own world, I knew I'd made a mistake."

"Then why didn't you come right back?"

"My parents, I made a promise to them."

"My daughter speaks the truth–as President and First Lady of the Republic of the United Kingdom, we have to be seen to be above reproach, and using The Gate is forbidden, yet we allowed our own daughter to violate laws we had helped write."

"What do you mean when you say The Republic of the United Kingdom?"

"There is no monarchy."

I could tell by his expression, it's too much to take in. "Can we discuss the finer details later?"

"No Royal Family?" he queries.

"Gone, but not forgotten," Mother replies. "It was the will of the people, but The Queen is still revered, even if she no longer occupies the position she once did."

"She still lives?"

"Oh, yes, and another difference to your world is we are more advanced with technology."

"I must see this place for myself."

"It looks a little different to what you see from your own window, but our science is leaps and bounds ahead of what you have here."

I'm suddenly suspicious. "Mother, you seem to know an awful lot of what this world is."

"After your last visit, sealed documents were opened, and we learned a lot more about previous crossings."

Thirteen - I See the Truth

I can't believe what I'm hearing but I know it's the truth. It's a lot to take in. No Royal Family, and the United Kingdom a republic. Never in a million years would I ever have guessed. I want to find something to discredit what I am being told but can't argue with what I just watched. It would be too elaborate a hoax to stage. Plus, seeing him with my own eyes tells me the whole truth.

"So there have been others who crossed over?"

"More than we were led to believe," Adriana answers. "Which is why The Gate was eventually sealed."

"Who created it?"

"Scientists concerned about global warming in our world found a way to manipulate a pathway through dimensions."

"Why bother?"

"There was concern about how much longer the Earth could sustain us."

"So, they created a portal to another world as a means of escape?"

"More to gather intelligence about your own world and at what stage of global warming you were at. They wished to see if your world had anything that might help ours."

"And what then?"

"People discovered The Gate through gossip, and while I'm not au fait with the technicalities, there is some sort of problem with two of the same existing in one place."

"A paradox?"

"It's a lot to get your head around but our scientists determined it too dangerous and petitioned parliament to discontinue research."

"Both you and Raven are here." The science of it all hurt my brain. "How do you know your doppelgangers, if that's even the right word, won't be affected?"

"Something about the two being in close proximity to the other."

"Well, whatever it is, you're both safe while here."

"I hope so," Raven said.

"And what of the rest of the world?"

"Vastly different to this."

"How?"

"New Zealand was consumed decades ago by a devastating Earthquake, and what was left of that once beautiful country sank into the ocean." She lowered her eyes to the floor for a moment. "Japan suffered the same fate ten years ago."

"My God." I feel sick at such a massive loss of life.

"It was devastating but there is more—"

"Mother, is it wise to tell him all of this?"

"You want Dalton to know the whole truth, and besides, Raven, you know our scientists finally discovered how to reverse the damage—our world is in better shape now than it was even five years ago."

Scientists can't bring the dead back, I tell myself. "What else is different where you come from?"

"The United States of America is no more."

I fear the worst, knowing the America I know, and love is populated with over three hundred and thirty million people. "Oh, no."

"Following a period of social upheaval, citizens rioted, which ultimately led to a second civil war, and the once unified states declared independence from one another."

"Shit!" It's like something from a disaster movie.

"But, as turbulent as that time was for our American friends, there has been a lasting peace over the years for them, and humanity as a whole. Famine is no more, war is a thing of the past and there are no homeless–as a civilisation we finally learned to put our differences aside to work together as one race no matter a person's age, race, financial worth, sexuality, or skin colour–we learned from our blinkered past, and while we do not wish to supress what was, what will be is the most important marker for our society. We look forward, and only glance back when there are further lessons to be learned."

"So, my son was born into a better world than exists here?"

"Who can say if that is true or not," Adriana replies. "We caught on eventually and so will this world. History is our greatest teacher; it enlightened us, and in time, it will do the same for everyone here."

"I'd like to think that will be the case."

"As would I."

"My world has many advantages, but we still suffer there as you do here with death, accidents or otherwise." Raven spoke with a tinge of sadness to her tone. "Technology has yet to find a way to restore life to the dead."

Thinking of such technology horrifies me. There is a cycle of life, and with that comes death. No human being has the right to tamper with that. *What about Raven crossing over?* I ask myself. "Our night together, was that simply you trying to convince yourself it was one last hurrah with the one you lost?"

"I hadn't anticipated spending as much time with you as I did–it was the goodbye I needed but in you I found so much more and over time, as that little boy grew inside of me, I was able to separate you and him. My Dalton was gone, but you were as far away as you could possibly be, still I couldn't forget you, then having Noah, the distance grew exponentially but all I wanted deep down was to be close to you again and for you to know your son."

"You didn't have to come back?" I realise the gift she has given to me in returning.

"No, I didn't," she replies. "I wanted to, and that is the difference, and for our son, not just me."

"I would never have known of his existence."

"Noah would ask questions and while my Dalton is lost to me, why would it be right for him to have lost his Dalton?"

Adriana sits next to me, places her hand on top of mine and taps it gently. "It wouldn't have been right, Raven, which is why your father took the steps he did."

"He moved heaven and earth, right?" I knew I would do the same for Noah.

"Yes, and at great political risk, but Raven is our only child, and we did what we had to do."

"So, what now?" I ask. "You return there, and I never see my son again." Part of me thinks it would have been kinder for me never to know.

"I confess, we did not think that far ahead," Raven admitted. "But there has to be a way."

"There is," Adriana answers swiftly and with a decisive tone.

"Which is," I query.

"You act as official advisor to President Phillipe Andre."

"And how would that work, and to a man I have never met?"

"We introduce you to parliament and create a role that allows you to travel through The Gate as and when you wish. But as part of that agreement, you will furnish our scientists with information about the progress of your world, in the hope we can step in and stop the calamities that befell ours from happening here."

"And that's it?"

"For now, yes."

"You have it all planned, don't you, Mother." It isn't a question, more an accusation. Raven has a knowing look in her eyes.

"Don't look at me like that, you know your father and I like to plan for any eventuality."

"So, I can return with you?"

"That was not agreed beforehand, or even discussed between my husband and I, but on this occasion, I will take the decision upon my shoulders and bugger the consequences."

"Father will not be happy."

"Your father can grumble all he likes, Raven, because I feel it imperative he meets the father of his only grandchild."

"So, I'm going back with you?"

"If that is your wish, yes." Adriana replies. And it is at that moment I see her for who she is. Yes, she might be First Lady, but I will never underestimate that position because she is the spine in that political marriage. Without her by his side, the President would still rule, but not as effectively. Adriana exudes glamour, but with that comes power and a persona than commands respect. I'm reminded of Eva Peron and wonder how the top job became theirs. I suspect Adriana is the driving force, even if others do not wish to see it.

I'm on my feet in seconds. "Let me get my coat."

"Hold on," Raven warns. "Mother, are you sure?"

"Perfectly sure, and we can send the signal and leave from here."

"The Gate works that way?" she asks.

"As long as the signal is received, we can enter the portal anywhere we wish, but we will always return to the same co-ordinates."

"I don't mind admitting how nervous I am."

"This is for Noah," Mother adds. "Heaven and Earth, remember!"

"Right!"

"The crossing is one hundred percent safe."

"I'll be fine, but I need to make a few phone calls, so people don't report me missing."

"You do what needs to be done and we will be ready. But we will leave from the patio area outside, just in case."

With a phone call made to my assistant to tell her I will be turning my phone off to concentrate on personal matters for a few days, I'm ready to go on the adventure of a lifetime.

"Are your affairs in order?" Adriana asks.

"They are, well I think so."

"You should be back in a few days, so there is nothing to worry about, Dalton."

Easy for you to say, I think to myself. *You've crossed dimensions before, this is my first time.* A few minutes later, the three of us are standing outside on the patio. Raven wraps her arms protectively around Noah. "Can I carry him?"

"It's better if you don't, the first time can disorient a person."

"Right!" Taking a quick glance across the spectacular views of Liverpool, I suddenly realise how connected I am to my home city. Briefly, I wonder if and when I'll return.

"Are you ready, Dalton?" Raven asks.

"No, but let's do it anyway."

"I'll send the signal after three," Adriana advises as my heart thumps in my chest. "One, two...three."

And with a whoosh, I feel a pull at the centre of my core, almost like I have been yanked off my feet. But it's not as violent as that. "Shitting hell." I open my eyes and can't believe what I'm seeing. Initially disbelieving of their story, and still uncertain what I would find, I'm exactly where they told me I would be. I don't feel the disorientation and lift my hands. "I feel fine."

"Are you sure?" Raven asks.

"Positive." I take Noah from his mother and hold him close to my chest, but I needn't worry because he is still sleeping. I glance behind me, to the darkness, the nothingness of where I just came from, then in front of me, only a simple metal walkway that leads toward a set of what I suspect are thick steel doors.

"I told you."

"Now is not the time for idle chit chat." Nervously, Adriana moves us along the walkway. "Phillipe will be along momentarily, and he will not be pleased to find we have returned with an uninvited guest."

"This is my fault, Mother, not yours."

"Blame is not important, darling, rules are, and between us, we have broken one that could cause long term ramifications for your father."

Just as she finishes, the doors slides open and a man I realise is Raven's father walks toward us. Another man scrambles close behind him and neither take their eyes off me. "If I hadn't seen him for myself, I'd never have believed the resemblance…" Then his voice trails off as realisation hits home. "Explain yourself right this minute, Adriana."

I hardly know her, but I do not imagine she will take kindly to being spoken to in such an abrupt manner.

"Well, hello to you too, Phillipe," she replies with great hauteur. "I missed you too."

"What on Earth have you done, Adriana?" He looks at the man standing next to him. "Gregor, please leave us, and not a word, do you hear?"

"That goes without saying, Mr President." With a nod toward Adriana and Raven, then to his boss, he scurries away.

"I took charge of the situation and did what had to be done…" she snaps, displeased to be put in the firing line or have her decisions questioned. "…and nothing more."

"You do realise his presence here could mean political suicide for us."

"Father, please, don't blame Mother, this is down to me."

"Your mother is First Lady and knows better than most what her recklessness could mean."

I'd had enough of their wrangling. This is about my son, not their political standing with an adoring public. "And I am Noah's father, so where he goes, I will follow."

With Dalton and Noah settled in my suite, I'm left to deal with the fallout between my mother and father.

"Of all the stupid things, Adriana," father rages at her then turns to me. "And you, Raven, going along with this madness."

I know why he is angry, and I'll try to explain it to him, but I won't feel guilty for putting the needs of my child first. "How could I leave him behind after telling him he has a son? I couldn't be that cruel."

Mother stepped in to try and soothe the situation. "It was I who made the decision, Phillipe, so if the axe must swing, I humbly kneel before it."

"Oh, hush with the dramatics, Adriana, you know the buck stops with me as President and not the First Family."

"The public do not need to know what has transpired."

"And how do I explain the doppelganger of my dead son-in-law next to me in official family photographs?"

"You lecture me about dramatics," she shot back with her customary eyeroll.

"What I say is not meant to be dramatic, but tell me, how do we explain the resurrection of our son-in-law, well, go on, I'm riveted at how you can explain him away."

"I am not suggesting Dalton remain here, but as we discussed, a role for him, where he is seen to be working for us, and the greater good of his world."

"That's everything wrapped up nicely in a neat silk bow, Adriana, but you know it is not how decisions are made in my government–this is a republic, and I am not a dictator."

"Then, Mr President," she adds with a snide tone, "put your case to your ministers but be a little shortcoming with the entire truth."

"Mother, you're asking father to lie."

"For the good of his family, and what better reason can there be?"

"Adriana, you ask a lot of me."

"No, Phillipe, I do not, but your grandson will thank you for it in years to come." She is clever by playing the family card.

Father seems almost defeated and unsure of what to do. I am not accustomed to seeing this side of him. "So, what do I do, tug on the heartstrings of the ministers and tell them Noah has a right to know his father?"

"Is that a lie?" Mother asks.

"No, it isn't but—"

"Before you work yourself up to a tizzy, answer me this one question…"

"Go on," Father replies.

"Who is the most important person in this world to you?"

"You know the answer to that already." He's losing patience with her, so whatever card she has left to play, it better be soon.

"Do I?"

"Yes, Adriana."

"Okay, I do, but I want you to tell me."

"Besides you, Raven…"

"And who else?"

"Noah, of course."

"Exactly, and you have said yourself how much joy Raven brought to our lives, so does Dalton not deserve to know how it feels too?"

I prayed he would agree.

"Well, yes, he does, but if I am to do this, I have to think carefully and strategically."

It's time I contributed more to this conversation. "Daddy, I don't want to tell you what to do, but I think what would be more prudent is for you to speak to Dalton first, then make your decision."

"Oh, Raven, my beautiful girl, if only you knew how losing our Dalton affected your mother and I."

"Do you think I hadn't noticed your own grief?"

"That boy meant the world to us, so I do know why you had to say your goodbyes to this other, but I confess it strange looking at that face again and not seeing the one we lost."

"Get used to it, my darling," Mother replies with a tender tone. "He is part of our lives now, whether it makes us uncomfortable or not."

"And this is what you truly want, Raven?"

"I want Noah to know his father."

He closes his eyes for a moment. "Very well."

I looked to Mother and noticed her eyes shining with unshed tears. "So, you'll speak to Dalton?" I ask.

"Yes, but I will not make a decision until we have had the opportunity to talk—I want to get the measure of this man before doing anything rash."

Fifteen - President, or Father?

Almost bursting with feelings of love, and the urge to protect, I stared at Noah as he slept. *My boy*, I thought to myself as a knock on the door pulled me from thoughts of this strange world and how I came to be here.

"Come in," I spoke in a quieter tone than usual, not wanting to wake my son. But loud enough for whoever knocked to hear me.

"Am I disturbing you?"

I pushed myself to my feet. "Not at all, Sir."

"Please, sit, I am not your President."

"I don't stand because of your position, but out of respect for you as Raven's father and the grandfather to my son."

I saw a flash of admiration in his eyes. "Well, that is most kind, but please take a seat, we have matters to discuss."

"Okay." I sat back down while he took the chair opposite me. His staring is uncomfortable, but I understand it. He sees the other Dalton when he looks at me. "You find it hard to look at me, don't you?"

"I always prefer honesty, and right now I don't know if I watch you with wonder and astonishment or abject horror."

"I get that."

"Do you?"

"Yes, I'm the spitting image of your dead son-in-law, and from a parallel world—Alfred Hitchcock couldn't make this shit up." I immediately regretted the use of profanity.

"Alfred Hitchcock you say?"

"Yes, do you know of him?"

"He was one of the greatest figure skaters this world has ever seen."

Things had just become more bizarre if that is possible. "A figure skater, wow."

"I shouldn't ask, but was he well known on your side?"

"Not for his dancing abilities, no."

"Ah…"

It couldn't hurt to tell him the truth. "He was one of England's finest and renowned Directors, as well as a producer and esteemed screenwriter."

"How interesting."

"I confess, I'd never thought of him in ice skates and tight lycra." I find it amusing and can't help but chuckle. "I'm sorry, but when I woke up this morning, this is the last thing I'd ever had guessed would be in store for me."

"When my son-in-law died, I grieved terribly, but Raven was my overriding concern, and in time, I leaned on the memories, but seeing your face brings it all back to me, and it seems I haven't dealt with his passing as well as I believed."

"There is no time limit on grief, Mr President."

"He was a good man, and call me Phillipe, please."

With a nod I acknowledge his request. "I am sure he was."

"And that isn't to say you are not, but aside from the physical side of you, I know nothing else."

"What is it you wish to know?"

"Are you a good man?"

"I try to be, yes, but I'm human and at times we make mistakes."

"Mistakes I can live with...Dalton." I noted how tentatively he used my name. "It is how a man recovers from them."

"If you are worried about my intentions to your daughter, I must be candid and tell you I haven't worked that part out."

"I see."

"Do you believe in love at first sight, Phillipe?"

"The sensible part of me says no, but the romantic in me says yes."

"Then you might understand when I say it is how I felt the moment I met Raven—that we were meant to be and spending the short amount of time together we did, I felt the connection, and while it may have been entirely different from my side, what resulted from that meeting is a new life, and while my feelings for Raven are confused, the welfare of my son is paramount."

"I respect your candour, young man, and as a father, I feel the same desire to protect and nurture my child as you do yours."

"You've hit the nail on the head, Sir. I did not come here to cause trouble, but to be with my son and to try and make some sense of this craziness."

"It is crazy, isn't it?"

"Oh, yes," I reply with a smile as Noah stirs then opens his eyes.

"Ah, the little tyke is awake."

"Raven told me you are yet to hold your only grandchild."

"I felt it right you had that honour before me."

"Well, that's no longer a concern, so..."

"Ah, I'm not so sure now is the right time."

"There is no better time for you to hold him."

"You don't mind?"

"I'd mind more if you didn't."

He stood up. "Very well." I shifted from my position as Phillipe swept in and carefully lifted Noah, then cradled him in his arms. The moment moved me more than I thought it would, but in his eyes, I saw unconditional love. "Hello, my little one," he whispered. "I'm your grandad." Raven had mentioned he was yet to hold his grandson. Then to my surprise, a single tear dropped onto the top of Noah's head. "I've been waiting a long time to hold you, but don't think for one moment, I haven't loved you because I have, with all my heart."

"You must have the magic touch."

"Do I?"

"He's gone back to sleep."

"I confess I have never known a baby as quiet as this one."

"Really?"

"Not even Raven was this easy to manage."

"He knows he is surrounded by people that love him."

"And now he has you, and it should be no other way."

"Do you know what you plan to do about all of this yet?"

I saw the light in his eyes. "I have an idea, but I have to tread carefully."

"May I ask what that idea is?"

"Of course. Just let me settle Noah and I will tell you what's on my mind." He returned the baby to his spot then pressed a call button on the table. A moment later, a female member of staff arrived. She couldn't hide her shock at seeing me. "Ah, Jennifer, will you please arrange for lunch to be served on the terrace, and gather all the staff, there are things I must say."

"Very well, Mr, President." With a quick glance, she rushed toward the doors before Phillipe stopped her.

"And, Jennifer, I expect total discretion in regard to my guest here."

"Of course, Sir."

Once she had left the room, I confided my fears. "What if she tells others what she has seen?"

"She won't, but I aim to announce your presence here as soon as possible."

"You're going to tell your people about The Gate?"

"Its existence is already in the public domain, but her reaction to seeing you has given me another idea, but I need to run it by Adriana, Raven, and you, of course, before I finally decide."

"I'm intrigued."

"It's quite simple really—Dalton has returned from the dead."

"And you think people will really fall for that?"

"If they believe he never really died in the first place, and that it was faked, then yes."

Another voice startled me. "Are you mad?" I turned to see Adriana leading the charge with Raven hovering in the doorway behind her. Their expressions are unreadable.

"Far from it, my darlings."

"It will never work, and parliament will never fall for it."

"Maybe not, but the public will because Dalton was very much loved, and if we spin it the right way, anything is possible."

I look at Raven. "How do you feel about it?"

"I don't know." She is desperately sad, and I want to comfort her." Walking toward her I hold out my arms. She falls into them as tears fall. "I don't like to hear you cry."

"What I feel for you is totally different to what I felt for him, and while I want you to be part of Noah's life, I can't live with this plan, it's not right. He was my husband, and I won't pretend you are him."

"Then what do you suggest?" Phillipe asks. "Tell me."

"We tell the truth, darling." Adriana casts an adoring glance at Noah then steps closer to her husband. "It is the only way, and if we lose power, our family remains intact, and no price can be put on that."

Quickly, he replied. "You are right." He focuses on Raven. "Forgive me for suggesting such a thing."

I let Raven go. She turned to Phillipe. "I know your best interests always lie with your family, but let's do it right." He nodded. "And you will know the truth, and that truth will set you free."

"John 8:32," I mutter.

"You know it?" Adriana asks.

"It's been a long time since I stepped foot in church, but some things are ingrained. Raven is right, the truth will set us free."

Sixteen - Separated at Birth

We sat around the table on the terrace. Lunch had yet to be served because my father wanted to make an announcement to his staff.

Dalton held my hand. "I'm scared," I admitted.

"Don't be."

"You told me Jennifer's reaction, what if the others speak out of turn?"

"They will not talk, not if they know what is good for them," Mother announces. "Besides, they all signed iron-clad non-disclosure agreements at the commencement of their employment at the palace."

My father takes his seat at the head of the table as scores of staff walk down the long marbled floored corridor toward us.

I hear whispers as they approach then notice Jennifer hovering at the back, looking shell-shocked.

All eyes are focused on Dalton. The more they look, the louder their mumblings become.

My father coughs to bring order to the proceedings. "Ah, thank you all for coming." Their focus remains on Dalton. "I realise seeing this gentleman sitting here is a shock, and while I want to explain to you all the how's and why's, I must ask for absolute discretion, because you all know scandal is the last thing any government needs or wants." We are greeted with silence and I don't know which way this is going to go. "I trust each and every one of you with this information and ask you allow me to inform my ministers that my son-in-law's identical twin brother, Dillon, contacted me some time ago and requested an audience." Gasps echoed about the terrace and I sensed their relief. "I have known about him since the sad passing of his brother, but out of respect I asked he keep his identity secret until such time I felt it proper to announce his existence." I looked at them as they eyed my father curiously. "You see, Dillon's birth mother died giving birth to them…" It is true that my Dalton was orphaned at birth and raised by adoptive parents, so this story isn't beyond the realms of possibility. "…sadly, the brothers were separated and neither knew of the other…" I watch as their expressions settle into one of calmness. "…it wasn't until seeing news coverage of Dalton's death that he did some digging and realised his parentage."

"It was quite a shock," I add. "But as fantastic as it is to meet a blood relative of my husband, it saddens me that Dillon will never know how wonderful a man his brother was." Looks of sympathy are fired my way. *We have them in the palm of our hands*, I think to myself.

It took some convincing that announcing Dalton as my deceased husband's long lost twin is the best course of action to take, but I have to agree, it was the right one to make.

"So, you see…" Mother takes over. "…we had to ensure that Dillon is the man he proclaimed to be, and to be respectful to the public because they too loved Dalton."

"But please remember, this is not a reason to be sad, only to celebrate."

"Do any of you have questions because now is the time to ask." It's only fair I give them this chance to talk. I look into their eyes, then Jennifer steps forward.

"May I?"

"Of course," I reply.

"Forgive me, but little Noah, is he the father?" Jennifer nods at Dalton.

"I don't think that is—

I interrupt my father. "Father it is fine, and I am more than willing to answer."

"I wish no disrespect."

"And none is taken, Jennifer, but in answer to your question, yes, Dillon is Noah's father." I watch as eyes widen. They hadn't expected me to confirm their suspicions. "But if you allow me a moment to explain—I was so lost in my grief, then out of the blue, I see his face, and believe I've been given the one thing we know can never be..." Jennifer dabs at her eyes. "So, you see, in my confusion, I fell into the arms of the one man I believed could take my pain away."

Dalton spoke up. "I know it isn't an ideal situation and I do not make a habit of falling into bed with women I have just met, but there was a connection between us—we leaned on one another for comfort and the result is Noah, and I won't apologise for him."

Mother stared them down. "Dillon's wish to be involved in his son's life and his presence at the palace forced us to reveal the truth. I hope you can forgive us, but we did what was right for our daughter and grandchild."

Jennifer opened her mouth to talk but an interruption we hadn't anticipated sent ripples through the assembled group.

"What the hell is this?" Jackson Myers stopped dead in his tracks and stared at Dalton.

"Jackson, what are you doing here?" Father asks, irritated by his unannounced and unwanted presence.

"Urgent matters to discuss, Mr, President, but I never—"

Mother cut in. "You are all dismissed but I remind you not to discuss what he has told you, and definitely not outside the palace walls until we are ready to make the announcement."

The staff scuttled away, and still Jackson focused on Dalton.

"I'd like to introduce you to Dillon, Dalton's twin brother."

"What have you done, Phillipe?" Jackson replied, accusingly.

"I have no idea what you are talking about, now what is this urgent business you wish to speak of?"

"Are you going to deny him being here is not the result in Raven passing through The Gate?"

"As I have already explained, this is Dalton's twin brother."

"Rubbish," Jackson hissed. "Dalton has no twin brother. We know because any person connected to the President and First Family is automatically vetted."

"He was adopted at birth, just like Dalton, and neither one knew of the other."

"Yet, he remains mute." Jackson addresses Dalton.

"Because I choose to."

"My God," he exclaimed, "they even sound the same."

"Twins often do, Mr, erm..."

"My name is Jackson Myers, and I am the Vice President."

"Your position is of no interest to me, nor is my personal family business." Dalton's stance impresses me.

"The child is yours I take it and you are the reason our revered President lobbied for his daughter to be given permission to cross through The Gate."

"You have such an imagination," I add. "Father wants me in that position because he trusts me."

"With respect, Raven, your father placed you in the position because it is the only way you could retain contact with him."

"And what of it?" Father snapped, losing patience with his Vice President. "Would you not have done the same for your daughter?"

"It was you who wrote the law and signed it into parliament, yet you circumvent it without worry."

"What do you intend to do?"

"Nothing if he returns to his world and remains there."

"And what of Noah?"

"He will never miss what he doesn't know."

Dalton pushed himself to his feet. "I won't leave my child, you pompous arsehole."

Jackson ignored the insult and turned back to my father. "You know him being here can cause untold trouble, and if confirmation of The Gate's existence is made public, hoards will rush the palace to seek out the same as Raven did."

"I'm sorry, Father." I had brought this crashing down on us.

"There is nothing to apologise for, Raven, and Jackson will keep his mouth shut, or find himself out in the cold, politically, that is."

"I will not allow you to fool the very people you promised to represent truthfully."

"What good will telling them do?"

"You do not know how him being here will affect us, or them on the other side. It is why we voted to send teams through, so we know the ramifications on both sides. It is not for you to use The Gate as you wish, Mr President."

"Then I will leave with Dalton, and never return."

"And what of their world? Of you taking the chance of meeting your doppelganger. You both cannot exist in the same place."

"We don't know that for sure Mr Myers," Mother adds. "It is purely guess work on our part."

He looks at her with sympathy in his eyes. "Forgive me, but are you really willing to take the chance of disrupting two worlds for one person?"

"That one person is our daughter," she replies.

"Send him back to where he came from and I shall say no more about it. But if you don't, I will inform the ministers of your actions and ask for a vote of no confidence and start removal proceedings."

"You wouldn't dare," Father raged.

"Don't test me, Phillipe," Jackson replies. "We have known one another for many years, and while you have my loyalty, so do the people and if something you do puts us all in jeopardy, it is my duty to inform them."

"Don't do anything foolish, Jackson," Father warns.

"Then do the right thing."

"Will you give us twenty-four hours to come up with a solution?" I ask. "For Noah's sake."

He mulls his answer. "For the child, yes, but he must return to his own world."

"And if I choose to go with him?"

"If you do as your father suggested, you may come and go as you please, as long as he stays where he ought to be."

"Will you keep my secret?"

"You have my word." With a nod toward my father and mother, he walks away. "One day, Phillipe, and no longer."

Seventeen - Tough Choices

Phillipe and Adriana left Raven and me to talk. There is a lot to discuss but I'm not on a level playing field. This city around me might have familiarity, but it's entirely different at the same time. I don't recognise the political landscape, nor can I get on board the breaking up of the United Kingdom with England as a Republic.

Everything I know seems to sit to the left of me, same time but in another place. It's the stuff of nightmares or a bad trip, and the longer I remain here, the more I am certain it is not my home, nor can it ever be. I feel out of place, and don't belong. But what of my son; born of parents from different worlds—not alien, definitely human, but at the same time, abhuman. *Where is Noah's place? Where does he fit?* These are all questions I ask myself. *Can he exist safely in either world?* I can't answer any because I don't know.

"What's on your mind?" Raven sits beside me and takes my hand. It feels good to touch her.

"Everything and nothing," I reply, gripping her hand tightly. "I don't know which way is up and down, or which Earth is the real one."

"Both are real."

"How?"

"The science is a complex issue and lost to me, but there are theories about a multiverse, that there are more versions of Earth than the two we know about."

I hold my head in my hands. "My brain aches."

"Don't worry about what you cannot control, Dalton."

"That's just it, Raven, everything is beyond my control—this world, how I exist in it, or don't, how you can exist in mine, then there is the most important person in all of this—Noah."

"We will do what is right for him, and if sacrifices have to be made, so be it."

"Is it really so easy?"

"He is our son and deserves to know both mother and father. That is how it will be, and I will settle for no less."

"You seem determined."

"My son's happiness is all encompassing and if I have to leave the world I know and make it elsewhere, it is a small price to pay."

"You'd really do that?"

"For him, without a shadow of doubt."

I didn't doubt her, but there is now the added problem of Jackson Myers. Would he stand by his word and allow me to return without consequence to Philippe and Adriana? Instinct tells me never to trust a politician, no matter where I am, that he will use it to gain a political advantage. "How well do you know this Jackson guy?"

"As well as any of my father's cabinet."

"So not well then?"

She grins. "Does anybody ever truly know anybody?"

"I feel I know you, well the essence of you, at least."

"As I do you, but as Father will tell you himself, politicians are a strange breed, and while they profess to work for the good of the country they represent, rarely is that the case—most are self-serving idiots or sycophants."

"But that didn't really answer my question, Raven."

"If you are asking if he can be trusted, my gut tells me no, that he will use what he knows to oust my father from the top job." She looks worried and releases my hand to wring hers together.

"So, what do we do?"

"Jackson is right about you not being able to stay here."

"If I go, will you leave with me?"

"If I left with you, where would I go?"

"You would stay with me of course."

"That is kind of you, but we are not set in stone."

"Raven, I'm rich beyond my wildest dreams and have more than enough to support you and Noah, and whether that is with us living in separate places or not, at least he will have us both in his life."

"I'm not closing my mind to a future with you, Dalton, but I made the mistake once of believing you could replace what I lost, and now I know, you might share the same face, but you are your own person, as was he."

"It's reassuring you see me for me, but the truth is, I fell in love with you the moment we met." Her shocked expression told me my truth isn't something she'd truly considered.

"You did?"

"I spent so much time searching for you, but you'd vanished, and it was like a dream, that I had imagined you and our night together."

She appeared sad for a moment. I saw the pain of her past reflecting back at me. "I'm so sorry. I hated leaving you like that."

"I understand, so there is no need to apologise, but whatever the future holds for us, I will always protect you as my friend and the mother of my son. I can't offer you anything more right now, but I'm a good person..."

"Don't you think I know that already?"

"I'm open to whatever the future brings, but this situation is one I never expected to find myself in, so I'm just going with the flow right now."

"I promise, we will find a way."

"Whatever happens, we all have to be happy, but I have niggling doubts that will happen."

"Explain your thoughts to me," she asks.

"Well, I am only one person out of place, whereas you and your parents belong here. Then we have Noah who is a child of both worlds…"

"I see what you mean, and while what you say is true, a way around these issues has to be found."

I wonder if she regrets seeking me out to reveal the truth. "I guess so…"

"Don't worry, Dalton—"

"I'm trying not to, but I feel a sense of dread."

"That's not good."

"No, it's not, but I truly feel trouble is approaching. Call it instinct or whatever you want but something is coming."

Raven snuggles into me, and while it feels good being this close to her, I can't shake my fears. I close my eyes, savouring this tender moment together, dreaming of what could be if destiny is kind to us. Then a loud rumbling sound snaps me back to reality. "What the hell was that?" Noah stirs and, for the first time, cries. Raven rushes to scoop him up. "Please tell me that noise is a regular occurrence here."

"I've never heard it before, but it sounded like it came from the lower floor of the palace."

The doors burst open, and Adriana comes toward us at speed. I can see anxiety in her eyes. Instinct screams at me. *Told you!* "We must go."

"Mother, what is going on?" Raven cradles Noah close to her chest.

"Jackson has betrayed us all, and we must get out of here."

"And go where?"

"Armed forces surround the palace, and he intends to have us all arrested, Dalton included."

"Me?" I ask, stunned.

"To use you as an example of what can happen when crossing The Gate."

"He would really announce its existence to wrestle power from Father?"

"That man would do anything to rule."

"We have to use The Gate and return to my world. We'll be safe there."

Mother looks at him. I can see the cogs turning in her mind. "Dalton, we still don't know if we would be safe there long term."

"But right now, we have no other option. I'll protect us all."

Phillipe dashes into the room. "We have to go, now. The palace guards will keep anyone out, but they won't hold out for long."

"This is madness, Phillipe—you are the President and should be able to explain to your people."

"It's a coup, Adriana, and Jackson is only interested in securing his own future—it's too late to do anything else, and if we resist, we will be shot."

"Can we get to The Gate from here?" I ask.

"Yes, but we run the risk of being caught."

"We have to try…"

"Sir, Madam…" Jennifer appears from a door behind us, and I wonder how long she had been listening before announcing her presence. "This way, please."

"Go," Phillipe ordered, as Raven led the way with Noah still in her arms. I put a protective arm around her as I caught up.

Through the door is a wide set of circular steps, but I have no idea where they lead to.

"Jackson has the Army on side and they're just about through, you have minutes to get out of here."

"How are we to escape?" Adriana asks.

"You should use The Gate, Madam," Jennifer replies. "We will hold them off for as long as possible."

"You know of The Gate?" I ask.

"We all do, Mr Dalton."

"I'm not Dalton."

She shot me a knowing look. "Not the one we loved, no, but a version of him…"

"You all knew?" Phillipe asked.

"Of course we did, Sir, right away. But we promised to serve and protect you and we will do exactly that."

"Thank you, Jennifer."

"It is my pleasure, now we must go because it won't be long until the Army tears the palace apart looking for you all."

"We can never thank you." Phillipe looks genuinely touched.

"Get safely to the other side, that is all we ask, Sir." We descend the stairs quickly and rush along a corridor then through another down and down a small set of steps. Another corridor and we are standing at the doors of an elevator. "This will take you to where you need to go."

"I'd forgotten about this route," Phillipe admitted.

Another rumble above tells me the Army has breached the palace walls.

"You have to go, right now." She presses the call button and the doors open.

"In, all of you," Phillipe orders, as we file in. He turns to look at his faithful staff member. "I can never thank you, Jennifer."

"Be happy, all of you." Phillipe kisses her on both cheeks. "It has been my honour to serve you all." He steps in as heavy footfall is heard close by. "Go, go, go," she urges as the first steam of armed forces charge down the corridor.

"Press the button, now," Raven yells.

The doors close as gunfire sounds. Stunned silence follows Jennifer's high-pitched screams as they open fire on her.

Adriana presses her hand against her mouth and cries muffled tears. But we are all too stunned to offer comfort.

The journey down seems to take forever but eventually the doors open, and I'm back in a familiar space.

"You have to stop the elevator from going back up, Phillipe." I'd seen enough action movies to know the score.

Eighteen - Everything Changes

Everything I think I know changes in minutes.

Dalton, my family, and I are now on the run with the only means of escape crossing The Gate into an uncertain future. There hasn't been time to study the effects of living on a parallel world, but we are left with no other choice.

Father destroys the control panel, rendering the elevator useless. But at least I am safe in the knowledge that if we can't get to the higher floors, nobody can reach us.

"Come along, Raven," Father urges, punching in the security code to the sealed room. Seconds later, the door swings open to reveal The Gate room, and inside an unwanted guest.

"I knew you would all find your way here eventually." Jackson Myers is waiting for us and points a gun at my father.

I stop in my tracks, fearful for my son's life. Dalton stands in front of us protectively. "Don't do anything silly, Raven."

"Jackson, you traitorous bastard," Father calls out.

With a confident air, he replies, "Stay where you are, Mr President..." A grin settles on his lips. "Well, soon to be our ex-Mr President, once the military incarcerates you and your power is stripped."

"I should kill you with my bare hands."

"I'm the one holding the gun..."

"Why?" Mother asks. "Have we not been good to you?"

"Because I can, Adriana."

"We trusted you." She condemned him with her tone.

"And that was your first mistake."

"The public will never accept what you have done here." I have rarely seen Mother so angry.

"I planned for this day long ago, to lead our once great country out of the Republic you continue to box us into, and back to the glorious imperial days when The Queen sat on the throne."

"All this, to reinstate the crown?" Father exclaims. "Are you mad?"

"To reunite this nation, England, Scotland, Northern Ireland and Wales, as it should always have remained."

"Unity is not the will of the people," Father reminds him. "Which is why we hold office."

"We are nothing while apart, Phillipe and you have been short-sighted not to have seen it."

I know my father believes we are better apart, but there has always been those in government who wished us to revert back to how it was in the old days. Little did any of us know, the Vice President was part of that rank of preservers. "Look what we have achieved in that time."

Myers isn't going to give in so easily. "But we lost so much along the way. Those things that made us great, all gone, and you rode that wave to power and glory and all the while hiding The Gate from your own people."

"I saw no reason to confirm anything."

"Because at heart, Phillipe, you are a dictator making decisions for the good of you and your family."

"I have never wished to dictate, only to lead our people to enlightenment, security and a better future."

I don't want to listen to them argue politics and their personal beliefs. "What is it you intend to do to us all, Jackson?" I ask.

"You and the innocent child cradled in your arms, will be banished to his world…" He gestured to Dalton. "And you can suffer the consequences if any, but his presence will not be tolerated here."

"Why not allow Phillipe and Adriana to come too?" Dalton asks. "There they are no threat to whatever it is you have planned."

"Neither are a threat to our future but they must answer for their crimes."

"Says who?" Mother asks.

"Says I." Jackson answers with authority.

"You are nobody to assert what you believe to be justice," I remind him. "And you would still be a nobody without my father holding you up."

"Is that so?" He points the gun at Dalton. I'm not fool enough to believe it is not loaded and ready to fire. "And what would you be without the doppelganger of your dearly departed?"

"Leave him out of it," I order, aware I have no standing. "My Dalton cared for you."

"And I used that to my advantage," he replies with a sly smile.

"What do you mean?"

"You didn't think I knew Phillipe was grooming him to rule at the end of his elected terms… well I knew and took steps to remove him from the equation."

"What did you do, Jackson?" Father asks, as all the clues fall into place like puzzles in a jigsaw. "Tell me you didn't…"

"I arranged for a simple accident, that's all, Phillipe, but he didn't suffer, well not much anyway…"

Emotions threatened to crush me. "You killed my husband, you evil bastard?"

"Not personally, dear Raven, but I admit the task was easy once I found the right man for the job."

"You are inhuman…" Mother accuses. "…and will burn in hell for your crimes."

"Hush, Adriana, your opinion is no longer of importance."

Anger grips me. To enable his rise to power, he ordered the assassination of my beloved husband, butchering a part of my heart with his heinous crime. "I'll kill you…"

"Well, hand the child to his father and let's see who has the upper hand."

"Jackson, no." Father moves quickly, and the bang echoes about the cavernous space.

Then with a thud he drops to the floor as blood pours from a wound in his abdomen.

Mother screams and rushes to his side. She drops to her knees and holds his face in her hands. "Phillipe…" she cries.

His eyes are closed. He doesn't move and I don't know if he is alive or dead.

I'm terrified and cannot move because my priority is to protect my child.

Jackson points the gun at Dalton. "Now is the time for you to take your leave, or else."

"I won't go, not without Raven and Noah."

"Then hurry, before I change my mind and shoot you all and throw you into the void."

"Raven…" He looks at me, but whatever words he wants to speak don't come.

"I won't leave my parents behind…"

"You must," Mother insists. I see the plea in her eyes. "It is too late for us, but I can meet my death knowing you and Noah are safe and happy."

I step closer to her and my father.

"Ah, Raven, I am sorry but there will be no touching goodbyes."

"Just one minute, I beg of you, please Jackson."

"No, leave now or stay and face the same fate as your traitorous parents."

"Raven, do as he says and go," Mother orders. "And remember we love you, no matter what."

"We must go," Dalton whispers.

My heart has shattered into a million pieces. I know I have to go but my feet are rooted to the spot. How can I leave my parents behind to face a certain death? I don't even know if my father is alive. I see no rise and fall of his chest. "I can't–"

Mother interrupts. "If you love us, Raven, then go, live your life and be happy."

"I love you so much."

"As we love you, but life is for living and now is your time, seize it."

"How touching," Jackson replies in a sarcastic tone. "Time is running out for you all, Raven. Go now while I still allow it."

The decision is taken from my hands as Dalton holds onto my arm and leads me along the walkway to The Gate. I step past my father and take one last look. My eyes meet Mother's, and in that last glance I try to convey everything she has meant to me. "I won't forget you," I whisper through tears.

I tilt Noah quickly, so she has one last look at him. With a smile she speaks, "Be happy, my darlings."

Then I'm pulled into the darkness and to a world I will always be a stranger in.

I tend to Noah and left Raven to sleep.

Weeks have passed since that awful day, yet her tears have not dried.

She feels their loss as though it is mere seconds ago and, as of yet, I have found no way to pull her out of the severe depression that has taken a stronghold of her.

I look into the eyes of Noah, the light of my life and am thankful every single day for the gift of his life. He is settled with me, but he needs his mother too. "Shall we go for a walk along the river? Would you like that, little man?" He looks at me and smiles and my heart melts. "Come on, let's get you ready and then we can come back and make Mummy some food."

"There's no need, I'm awake."

I turn to see her standing behind me. She's dressed and has finally brushed her hair. Could this be a turning for her, and us all? "How are you?"

"Tired, but I can't spend my life in bed, not when I have Noah to care for."

"He's safe with me."

"I know, but I need him right now."

"I get it, and we were just going to get ready to go for a walk, would you like to come?"

"Where to?"

"Along the river, if you fancy it?"

"I'm not sure…"

"Come on, it will do us all good, and you can't stay cooped up in here forever."

"It seems wrong living my life when they don't have theirs." They are her parents, and I understand why she feels the way she does, but life goes on, whether we want it to or not.

"Your mother and father gave their lives for you and Noah, don't make their deaths in vain." I hated to say these words to her for a number of reasons, but also because, neither of us knew for sure what fate Phillipe and Adriana met. "Do it for them."

She remained silent for a few seconds, then spoke, "Okay, but let's not go too far."

"Whatever you want."

Now is a good time for me to tell Raven I have purchased a property out of Liverpool. Being in the city didn't seem the right place to raise a child, and certainly not in a penthouse. There will come a time Noah will want to run around, ride a bike, play football, do whatever makes him happy, but this isn't the right setting for him. Money is no object and the beautiful six bedroom house with acres of ground surrounding it seemed too good to pass up. So, I made an offer, and later that day, it was mine, well, ours. "Shall we grab a bite to eat while we are out?"

"Yes, that sounds nice."

"Fish and chips?"

"Lovely." She hasn't eaten much these last weeks and has lost weight, so I feel some relief to have her agree to my suggestion. "I'll get Noah ready while you grab our coats."

The sun is shining, and the fresh air feels good against my skin. "This is nice," she says, closing her eyes as the breeze drifts in from the River Mersey."

"Yes, it is, and thank you for agreeing to come."

"I lay in bed last night and realised I had stopped living and it's the last thing my parents would have wanted. But you know, the realisation I will never know what became of them tortures me."

"You're not the only one." I hadn't admitted it to her, but I had flashbacks to that day, of watching Phillipe take a bullet from somebody he trusted. That last quick look at Adriana haunted me. Neither of them deserved such betrayal, but no action I can take can ever remedy it. I have to move on with my life and believe their suffering was minimal.

"Do you think of them often?"

"Every day I say a prayer for them, that somehow, some way, they are safe and happy and missing us as much as we miss them."

"Wouldn't that be something?" And for the first time, she smiles.

"Yes, it would,"

"But it cannot be, no matter how much I wish it."

We continued our walk along the promenade behind the Albert Dock. "Think of the good times, Raven..." Then without realising, we are back to the most special of places. Love Locks at Albert Dock. "Wow, it feels like a lifetime since we were last here."

"Something about this place soothes my soul."

"Mine too."

She kneels down to talk to Noah in his buggy. "This place means a lot to your daddy and I, and perhaps one day, you will bring the love of your life here and leave a padlock…" He looked up at her and smiled. "Wouldn't that be lovely, Noah." He gurgled his agreement. "You're Mummy's special boy, and I love you very much." She kissed his cheek, then looked up at me. "And you too, *my* Dalton."

I'm taken aback because it's the first time she has said anything like it. "You love me?"

"I never realised how much until now."

I hold my hand out. She takes it, and I pull her toward me, and into my arms. "I love you too, but you already know that."

"I wanted to tell you sooner, but my mind was a mess. It still is, but the clouds are parting finally, and I can feel sunshine once more."

"I'm glad, and despite the past, we can be happy."

"I know, but the city unnerves me, and I find looking from the penthouse onto familiar surroundings pulls me back to a dark past I am trying to step out from."

"Then my news should make you happy."

"Oh?" She pulled back a little, but my arms were wrapped around her waist.

"I closed on a new property, six bedrooms, a huge garden for Noah to play in and surrounding grounds."

"Oh my…"

"And the best news, it's not in the city, but out in the country. Not too far, but far enough away for you to be able to relax."

The joyous smile lit up her face. "Are you serious?"

"Yes, I was always going to tell you, but when I felt you were ready."

"It's the best news." She wrapped her arms tightly around my neck and our lips met. Just like the first time, energy coursed through us. Then, ideas of our impending move took hold. "When can we leave?"

"In a couple of weeks."

"So soon?"

"We can delay if you'd like?"

"No, no," she replies. "That suits me, I was expecting you to say months."

"I'm having a new kitchen fitted and some general work done, anything else can be sorted once we're in there, but it's ours."

"Do I have any right to feel so happy?"

"Yes, you do, and don't ever feel guilty for it."

"Oh, Dalton, I have so many plans for us."

"That makes me happy to hear, and to know you're going to be somewhere you feel safe if I have to go away for meetings."

"Noah and I could always come with you."

"Yes, you could, but remember, we still have to be careful your doppelganger here never learns of you."

"If she exists here…"

"I'm working with a Private Investigator now, just to see what I can find out."

"Be careful not to reveal too much."

"I won't, but until then, we need to keep you under the radar."

"I need a change of image…perhaps a new hair colour to start with."

"That might be an idea although I love you as you are."

"If it keeps the wolf from the door, it's a small price to pay, and besides, you're in the public eyes and if your tabloids are as horrible as ours were over there, it won't be long until my face ends up in the papers."

"That's quite true."

"So, let's head to the shops and get what I need. It's time I had a look around and took note of the differences instead of seeing shadows of my former home."

"Are you sure?"

"Perfectly sure, but before we go, can I ask a favour?"

"Anything, Raven."

"Dance with me."

"What, here, in public?"

"Why not? Where better than the here and now?" It's like history repeating itself. But I won't turn her down, not ever. "Okay!"

Seconds later, we are one and it doesn't seem to matter to either of us that others may be watching. We sway under the rays of the sun and the breeze from the Mersey, lost in one another's arms, but there is nowhere else I'd rather be.

Three weeks later, after one last sweep of the Penthouse that has been my home, I step into the elevator for the last time. The doors close and when they open, I step out into the foyer and into the path of Forbes, the trusted night concierge.

"I hadn't expected to see you," I admit, but secretly I am pleased to say goodbye.

"It is early, but I wanted to wish you well, Mr Delaney."

"You came just to say goodbye."

"It has been my pleasure to assist you these last few years and wherever life's journey takes you, I wish you, Miss Andre and little Noah all the happiness in the world."

"That is very kind of you, and I am so glad you were kind enough to come in early. But I had left a letter for you at your desk."

"Oh, really?"

"Yes, and while I don't have time now, in the letter you will find the offer of a job…"

"A job?"

"Yes, as my Personal Assistant."

"I am honoured, Sir."

"Have a read and see what you think. My contact details are included, and should you be gracious enough to accept, I shall be waiting."

"I don't know what to say." He is genuinely moved.

"Say yes."

"May I look through your offer and call you tomorrow?"

"Of course, and there is no rush, but the job is yours if you want it."

"Thank you, Mr Delaney."

"Shall we hug it out?"

"Ah, erm, well…"

I pull him into a hug, hopeful he will decide to join me. I hold him at arm's length. "I'll be awaiting your call, Forbes."

"Tomorrow at the latest, you have my word."

"I shall look forward to it."

"Well, goodbye for now."

"Until we meet again, Mr Delaney, your car is waiting."

"Thank you, my friend." With a heavy heart but excitement for what the future brings, I turn and walk away. Stepping through the doors, I clumsily slam into a guy entering the building. "Oh, gosh, I'm so sorry."

He dusts himself down, and for a moment, I'm caught by familiarity. "Forgive me, it's my fault."

"No, really, I was preoccupied and not watching where I was going."

"Well, no harm done, Mr…"

"Dalton Delaney. And your name is?"

"Mr Stone."

"Well, please accept my apologies, Mr Stone, but I should go. I have a car waiting to take me to my new home."

"Ah, how exciting."

"It is."

"Are you married?"

"Not yet, but we have a child together, and we're happy, so the big question is not far off."

"Well, that is wonderful."

"Quite!"

"I shall not keep you any longer, but I wish you the very best for the future and hope good things come your way very soon."

"Thank you." *What a lovely man*, I think to myself, before rushing away. He did seem familiar but when I turn to look again, I don't see him. But right now, I don't have time to mull over the possibility we had met somewhere before, and slide into the back of the car. "When you're ready," I say to the driver.

Seconds later, he pulls away and I'm on my way to my new life with the family I love.

Twenty - Ghosts of the Past

Country living is certainly different to what I am used to, but city life reminded me of everything we lost that day five years ago. Now, even though I know I will never get over the past, I've found a new happiness in a world I still consider strange.

This new pace of life suits me, and despite my husband's fame I keep out of the limelight, happy to play wife and mother to Noah, and six-month-old Daisy Adriana. The joy those little beings bring to my life is incalculable. While Dalton wows Hollywood, I keep things ticking over here. He's never away for more than two days at a time, something we agreed on way back, a promise he has never broken.

He's in the city at a meeting with our accountants and will be home any time.

I check my reflection in the mirror and still find the reflection that stares back at me surprising. I'm no longer blonde. The colour of my hair matches my name—raven, jet black, but it suits me, as does the new colour palette of makeup I now prefer. But hair and makeup are not the only changes to my appearance—a simple nose job altered my face enough not to draw comparisons to the other me. We now know she is out there, but there's no way our paths will cross, not unless I seek her out, which is something I'd never be foolish enough to do. I won't tempt the fates and put the mysteries of the universe to its ultimate test.

I hear Noah laughing in another room and wonder what mischief he's up to now. He's a good boy but shows no fear of anything.

Could life be any more perfect?

I bask in my surroundings, at my gorgeous home and realise once more I have everything I need, but not everything I want.

The death of my parents continues to haunt me–visions of my father lying with blood oozing from a gunshot wound plague me and no matter how I force them out of my mind, they come back with renewed vigour. I will never know what became of them, and that is the worst part.

"How are you today, Miss Raven?"

Forbes enters the kitchen, his usual jovial self and pulls me to the present. "Very good, and how are you?"

"Master Noah keeps me busy."

"He adores you I hope you know that." Their bond is a special one to behold.

"As I do him.

"Still, you shouldn't let him tire you out."

"I'm still a youngish man of forty something," he jokes, "so there's plenty of life in me yet."

"I know, but still, you took a position as Dalton's personal assistant and not childminder."

"Spending time with him is my pleasure because, raised in the foster system, it's the first time I feel like I have a family."

"You do have a family, us, and don't forget it."

"Thank you, Miss Raven."

"We'd be lost without you." My words are true. In the last five years, Forbes has become a part of our growing family. So much so, we confided in him the absolute truth of where I came from. He took it all in his stride, but I'm not sure he truly believed us, and thought it a plotline of Raven's Return, the best-selling sequel to Raven's Ghost.

Still, loyalty cannot be bought, and Forbes continues to show us the wonderful man he is. "Since I lost my parents, I've struggled to find people I can bond with, but right away, I felt like I could be myself around you."

"And you can, always," he replies, as Noah zooms into the kitchen on his trike, almost crashing into the cupboard doors.

I flinch, waiting for a crash that never comes. "Noah, please be careful." He is a typical boy and seems to have no fear of anything while I live on my nerves when he roars around the place at breakneck speed.

"Sorry, Mummy," and off he goes again. "Love you," he calls out in his cute voice.

"Love you too, darling, but not if you break my favourite vase." I am joking of course. Nothing could ever diminish the love I feel for my family. I watch him adoringly and realise how lucky I am. "That child will be a Formula One driver, I'm certain of it."

Forbes chuckles and gazes fondly as Noah disappears around a corner. "I confess he is the most adorable little one, as is little miss."

"I wish my parents could see them both."

"I am sure they can, if you believe in the afterlife."

"Well, nobody would ever believe parallel worlds exist and they do, so I guess anything is possible."

"Erm, quite." He shuffles uncomfortably, then does what he usually does when my parents are discussed. "I have matters to attend to."

"Oh, Forbes, before you go, has Noah said anything else to you about this imaginary friend of his?"

"Not for a few days, no."

"Good." I've been worried, but Dalton reminds me it's perfectly natural for a child as inquisitive as Noah to conjure things in his mind, even a friend that isn't there. He might take after his father and write blockbuster novels and screenplays for a living.

"Try not to be concerned, I hear a lot of children have imaginary friends."

"Yes, I've read up on it, and hope it's not because he's missing something in his life." *He is… his grandparents.*

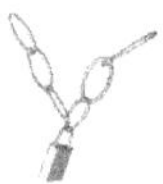

Later than evening, after her feed, I settle Daisy into her cot. She's the most angelic child and reminds me of my mother. They share the same features, and it makes me miss my mum more. *I still think about you*, are words I send out into the universe every night, hoping by some miracle, she hears. *You too, Father.*

Dalton appears at the door. "Noah is asking for you."

I turn to answer. "I'm coming," I reply, then peer over the cot at my sleepy little girl. "Goodnight, my angel."

I usually like to watch her fall asleep, but Noah won't settle unless I say goodnight to him, and I'm anxious to spend some alone time with my husband.

Daisy is safe and secure. Her nightlight is on, casting images of teddy bears onto the walls and ceiling. It plays a tune that settles her, and she won't sleep at night without it. For such a young age, she already knows her mind.

I turn the baby monitor on but still leave the door ajar, then head across the landing to Noah's room.

He's lying on his bed with his hands behind his head. "I've been waiting a long time, Mummy."

Dalton grins. He is beyond proud of his clever son.

"Have you now?" I play along.

"Yes, Mummy, I have."

"Well, I am sorry, but I'm here now to tuck you in."

"Do you want to get in with me?"

"Not tonight because you've been very tired today, so I think a long night's sleep is in order, especially if you want to go to the zoo tomorrow."

"I like the zoo."

"Oh, I know you do and if you stay in your bed, rather than climbing in with us, we can spend the whole day there, and if you want, you can have your face painted."

"It's a deal," Noah replies, as Dalton sniggers.

"Inky Dinky Pinky Promise." I hold my little finger up.

I link mine into his. "Promise!"

"Deal," I confirm. "Zoo it is, now give Mummy a hug then close your eyes and drift away to dreamworld."

"I like it there."

"Do you?"

"Yes, my friend lives there."

"Does he really?" I look to Dalton and remember his words. I won't worry because it's just a little boy's overactive imagination.

"Yes."

"Does your friend have a name?"

"It's a secret, Mummy."

"Is it?"

"I'm not meant to tell you."

I feel uncomfortable, like there's a ghost in my house. "But you want to, don't you?"

"If I tell you, promise you'll keep it a secret."

"Squirrels' honour." The Squirrels are a sub-division of the Scouts, but for four to five year olds.

"Silly Mummy." He is in the Squirrels but there are no girls in his group. "You can't be in my group, you're too old."

"Well, I never." I tickle his tummy. "Mummy might cry, but not if you tell me the name of your friend."

"Can I whisper it to you?"

"Go on then." I lean in as he whispers a name into my ear. I zip a finger across my lips which tells him they are sealed. "Our secret, okay."

"Yes, Mummy."

"Right, time for sleep." I kiss his forehead. "Love you, my little angel."

"Love you too, Mummy, and you Daddy."

"Goodnight. Noah, I love you too."

Twenty one - The Mysterious Mr Stone

We settle on the squishy sofa in the living room and sip from red wine Forbes has kindly poured for us. "That was a very clever way of getting him to tell you the name."

"It still worries me, Dalton, all this talking to people that aren't there."

"He's got an over-active imagination, that's all."

"What if it's something else?"

"Like what?" I ask, not wanting to indulge these crazy thoughts.

"I don't know, they're not normal children, we both know that."

"We come from different worlds, but that won't have anything to do with this friend of Noah's, I guarantee it."

"Well, whoever this Mr Stone is, he keeps Noah awake at night."

I felt the thudding of my heart. "What did you just say?"

"What?"

"The name..."

"Mr Stone, that's the name of his imaginary friend." She can tell I'm spooked. "Why, what's up?"

"The day we left the Penthouse, you'd gone on ahead with Noah, and I'd said goodbye to Forbes and told him of the job offer, then when I walked out of the main doors, I think I told you, I slammed into a guy and something about him seemed familiar."

"Yes, I remember you telling me, but what of it?"

"His name was Mr Stone."

"You're kidding me."

"No, I'm not." Instantly, I'm on high alert and my mind takes me to places I'd rather not go. "You don't think…?"

"You said he seemed familiar."

"I've often thought of him, but I can't place where…"

"Stone, Stone," she says repeatedly, then I see the lightbulb moment as something comes back to her. "Gregor Stone."

"Who's he?"

"My father's assistant."

"Oh, God, yes, that's where I'd seen him before." *Shit!* "The day I arrived he was with your dad…"

She couldn't hide her terror. "That means Jackson Myers knows where we are, especially if Stone is communicating with Noah."

"We have to get out of here." I jump to my feet and hold my hand out for Raven. She takes it and I pull her up. Panic rests in her expression. "You sort Noah and I'll get Daisy."

"But, Dalton, where will we go?"

"I don't know, but we can't stay here."

"Do you think we're in danger?"

"This Mr Stone has been speaking to Noah, and there has to be a reason why." I didn't know what to do first. But I decide we need help. "Forbes…quickly…." I know he's in the kitchen.

He rushes into the room. "What is it?"

"We have to get out of here."

"But why?"

"They've found us…"

"Who?" Forbes asks.

"The people we told you about."

"From the other side?"

"Yes," Raven replies. "We have to get the kids out of here now."

"Calm down, Miss Raven, please."

"I can't, not when my family is in danger."

"They aren't," he said, reassuringly. "I promise you that."

I'm ready to spring into action. "You don't know that, Forbes."

"Yes, Sir, I do. And if you would settle down for a moment, I will tell you how."

"Forbes..." Raven stared at him, seemingly unsure of what to think. "What is going on?"

"Your parents are alive, Miss Raven."

I felt sucker punched by this revelation. "How do you know that Forbes, and be clear about it?"

"Mr Stone was sent through The Gate by your parents after the failed coup."

Raven slumped onto the sofa. I found a spot next to her before my legs gave way. "And you've known all this time?"

"The day you left the penthouse, Mr Stone approached me. At first, I thought him a fantasist, but he took my hand and suddenly I was somewhere I didn't recognise."

"My God, he took you to the other side," I exclaimed as Raven sat in silence.

"Yes, Sir, but I was sworn to secrecy until such a time it was safe for your parents to cross and be reunited with you."

"And now?" Raven asks."

"Jackson Myers disappeared and for a time we feared he had crossed over, but he was discovered hiding out in the Republic of California and was executed shortly after."

"When was this?" I ask.

"A few days ago."

"Were you ever going to tell us?"

"No, Miss Raven, my job was to protect you all until your parents revealed themselves to you."

"They're really alive?"

"Very much so."

My head is spinning.

"But my father, Jackson shot him."

"I don't know the exact details, but your parents can explain for themselves."

"How?"

"With this." He shoved his hand in his pocket and retrieved what looked like a mobile phone.

"What is it?"

"My way of communicating with your world."

"And you've had it all this time?"

"Yes, I have."

I didn't know whether to punch him or hug him. "And this Mr Stone, why has he been communicating with Noah?"

"Simply to get the child to trust him should he be called to whisk the children away to safety."

I completely understood that way of thinking, and turning to Raven, in tears, she might not be so forgiving. "They're alive, Dalton, all this time, they've been there while I grieved."

"Don't hate them, Miss Raven because they stayed away to protect you, until all danger had passed."

"They love you too much to put you, or our children at risk, you know that." I try to make her see sense. "Forbes is right, don't hate them for putting us first."

"I've missed them so much."

"Then tell them." Forbes holds the communication device out for me to take.

"What do I do?"

"Take it and press the green button, they'll hear you."

"Is that it?"

"Yes, Miss Raven."

"Take it, sweetheart."

"I'm scared."

I take it from Forbes. "And it's safe for her to contact them?"

"Yes, Sir, it is."

"Then why have they not contacted us?" Raven asks.

"Putting their affairs in order is all," Forbes replies. "Press the button and summon them."

"Here," I urge. "Take it and call them, it's what you've always dreamed of."

"It is." Her face crumples and she dissolves into tears. "But I'm scared it's not real and I'll lose them again."

"Then let me," I volunteer.

"Will you?"

"For you, anything." I hate to see my wife in so much pain.

"Now?"

She nods her agreement, and I can see she has held her breath.

I press the button and hear a crackling.

"Speak into it, Sir," Forbes advises.

I do as I am told. "Hello." I feel silly, like I am talking into a child's walkie-talkie. "Can you hear me?"

"We can." I'm almost overcome hearing the voice I recognise. "Do you hear us?"

"Yes, Adriana…"

"Raven, are you there?" I hold out the device to her, but she shakes her head. "Raven, if you can hear me, speak to me, please."

Tentatively, she takes it from me and holds it to her lips. "Mother… is it really you?"

"Oh, my darling, I've missed you so much."

She dissolves into floods of tears, and I can't hold my own back either.

Then, Adriana speaks once more. "I'm sending Mr Stone across now."

And in a flash, the man from my old building appears in my living room.

With a nod of greeting, he speaks. "It is good to see you again, Miss Andre, or is it Mrs Delaney now?"

"I can't believe this."

"I wish to apologise to you both for any subterfuge, but it was my job, and that of my friend, Forbes, to make sure you and the children were safe and that when the time came, your parents could come through The Gate and reunite with you."

Twenty two - As Life Should Be

Life will never be the same again, but it will be better than before because my beloved parents are alive and well. In a few moments, I will see their faces again.

I speak into the device and hear static and crackling. "Mother, do you hear me?"

"Yes, Raven," Mother replies. "We can."

"We are ready for you."

"Father will join me momentarily..." Then there is silence.

"Mother...?" More crackling. "...Mother, are you there?" The sound of silence terrifies me. "Mother, Father, if you can hear me, please answer."

"We hear you, Raven, and see you." I spin around at hearing my Father's voice and feel his presence.

They haven't changed a bit, and I take a moment to drink in their faces. How I have missed them. I can't hold my emotions in and look at Dalton who is crying.

Tears run down my parents' cheeks, then they open their arms. I rush toward them and fall into their embrace.

"Are you really here?" I ask through tears.

"Yes, Raven, we are," Father answers.

I look into his eyes and feel his love. "I thought I'd lost you forever."

"Not for forever, just a little while," Mother adds, kissing my cheek. She turns to Dalton and holds out her hand. "Come here, you gorgeous boy." He accepts her invitation and is enveloped in our hug. "We have missed you both."

I look over to Forbes and Mr Stone. Both dab at their eyes with matching handkerchiefs.

I hear the pitter-patter of tiny feet then his high-pitched voice. "Mummy, the noise woke me up."

My parents gasp at seeing their grandson for the first time in years. How he has grown. Breaking away from the huddle, I rush over to Noah. He doesn't appear to have noticed Mr Stone. "Oh, I'm sorry, sweetheart, but we have guests come to visit."

"Hello, Noah." Mr Stone steps forward. "It is way past your bedtime."

"Hello Mr Stone, have you come to tuck me in?"

"If that is your wish, then yes."

"Mr Stone may tuck you in but first I'd like you to say hello to some very special people."

"Who?"

"Would you like to say hello?" Dalton asks, approaching.

"Yes."

"Come to me." Dalton opens his arms and Noah jumps into them. "And let me introduce you to your Nana and Grandad."

"You told me they were in Heaven."

"We thought they were, but we were wrong."

It is too much for him to comprehend. But when he is older all will be explained.

"Hello, Noah," Father says first. "It is wonderful to see you again."

"Say hello," Dalton says soothingly.

"Hello, Grandad."

He is robbed of words for a moment, then as usual, Mother sweeps to his rescue.

"Now say hello to Nanna." She holds her hands to her mouth.

"Hello, Nanna, you're very pretty."

"Oh, my little darling boy, it's so good to see you." She holds her arms wide open. "Could I have a cuddle?"

Noah looks to me. I nod, giving him the go ahead he is looking for. "Okay," he says in his sweet voice. Then, being the boisterous little boy he is, he charges and rushes into her arms, almost knocking her off her feet. Steadying herself, she holds him tight, covering him in kisses. "You're the most handsome little boy I have ever seen."

"Am I?" he asks, always happy to be praised.

"Oh, yes, cross my heart," she replies, kissing him some more.

"What about me?" Father asks. "Do I get a hug too?"

Noah holds out his chubby arms. He is clever for his age and must sense neither mean him any harm. It's my father's turn now. "Wow, you're a big boy now."

"Am I?"

"The last time we saw one another, you were a tiny baby."

"Like Daisy?"

I forgot they had never met their granddaughter. It pained both of them, I could see it in their eyes. "Yes, just like your sister."

So engrossed in my own happiness, I hadn't noticed Dalton leave the room.

"And here is the little lady herself."

It is only then I notice Forbes and Mr Stone are nowhere to be seen.

"Oh, my..." Mother is stunned.

"She loves her sleep I'm afraid..."

He crosses the room and passes Daisy to his Nanna. "What a precious jewel she is, and just like Raven at her age." I can see the love my mother has for Daisy instantly. "Phillipe, look at her."

Father's eyes shine with tears, but his arms are wrapped around Noah. His time with Daisy will come soon enough.

"Mother, Father, please, sit down before you fall down."

Mother is the first to sit but can't take her eyes off Daisy. "I'm mesmerised by this little girl."

"I think Phillipe can say the same for Noah," Dalton adds.

"In my darkest times, I never for one moment thought I would make it here."

"But we did," Mother adds, lifting the mood. "Thanks to our friends on the other side."

"What happened, Adriana?" Dalton asks the question I have been desperate to ask.

"Well, the brief story is; Jackson attempted to overthrow the government with my military but what he didn't bank on was their loyalty to The Queen."

"The Queen?" I hadn't expected her to have any part in this. "She helped you?"

"Our people spoke, and it was their will to restore The Queen to her throne." As a staunch supporter of the Republic, I know this change will not sit well with him. "The Republic is no more."

"Oh, Father, I am sorry."

"Don't be, because it is only the intervention of The Queen, and her bringing order that I am sitting here with you today."

"I thought you were dead." I still shudder at the memory.

"Luckily for me, Jackson is a crap shot and he missed all major organs."

"You were lucky," Dalton says. "I don't mind admitting I thought you were a goner."

"It'll take more than that imbecile to finish me off."

"So, what now, Father? If you are no longer President, how were you able to cross over?"

"The Queen always liked me and requested I run for the position of Prime Minister, which is what I did."

"He won by a landslide," Mother added, proudly.

"And rightly so," Dalton added. "You are a good man, Phillipe."

"Thank you, my boy."

I'm only just aware that Noah has fallen asleep in my father's arms. "Do you want me to take him?"

"I've waited a long time to hold him again, leave him be." He kissed the top of his head.

Mother is transfixed by Daisy, who has finally opened her eyes. "Well, hello, my little cherub, I'm your Nanna, and I'm going to be around to watch you and your brother grow up."

"Are you, really?" I ask, scared to believe my parents can remain in my life.

"Special dispensation from The Queen, and that invitation extends to you all."

"Even me?" Dalton queries.

"The public are aware of the existence of The Gate and they know what happened to Raven—there are no more secrets left to tell."

"Oh, thank goodness." For the first time in years, I feel weightless.

"A lot has happened since we last met, and in a few weeks, I shall be sitting down with your world leaders to discuss our scientific advances, and to try and stop what happened in New Zealand and Japan from happening here."

"Amazing..." I reply. "And what about you Mother, what have you been doing with your time?"

"I left the life of politics behind a while ago, Raven."

"You did?" I'm stunned as she thrived on her position as First Lady. "Why?"

"Because without you, life wasn't the same..." I saw a flash of pain in her eyes and decided not to push the issue.

"Family means more to your mother and I than any position," Father adds, kissing Noah tenderly on the forehead.

Dabbing at the corner of her eyes with a silk handkerchief, Mother clears her throat then still choked with emotion, speaks. "Yes, Phillipe, family is everything... it's written in the stars."

The End

A Note from the Author

TRUE LOVE WINS EVERY TIME.
If you want it enough.
If you are one of the lucky ones to find an everlasting love...
Hold on tight and enjoy the ride!

Thank you for reading my words and taking the 'LOVE LOCKS' series to your heart.

I hope you enjoyed reading it as much as I did writing it.

It belongs to you now...

DHANI
x

'LOCKDOWN LOVE'

"Nothing has to change. It's not as though it's the first time I've kissed a guy."

As the world is held in the grips of a global pandemic, straight, handsome, athletic builder, Damon Boyd, is forced into lockdown.

His only company is gay, primary school teacher and housemate, Joey Reynolds.

Bonding over their love of superhero movies and buoyed by their shared love of good food, drink and company, harmony exists between the pair.

As time passes, growing anxieties force Damon permanently behind closed doors, leaving Joey to take care of everyday chores outside of the house.

But while sequestered, their friendship grows, and a spark is soon ignited between them.

Only Joey has the courage to fully acknowledge the change in dynamics, yet stealing a drunken kiss pushes them further into friend zone.

Damon refuses to admit what he is truly feeling, and believing the best way to re-assert his sexuality, he takes a risk that could have devastating consequences for them both

'THIS HEART WILL LOVE AGAIN'

"Place your hand over my heart, feel it's rhythm, and tell me it doesn't beat only for you."

One cold winter's night, fate delivers happily married Serena Tate a cruel blow, shattering her heart into a million pieces.

Such a devastating loss renders her unable to deal with the outside world, but a chance meeting guides her toward a new path—one that can offer comfort not just to her, but to those also struggling emotionally and psychologically.

Haunted by lost love, Serena must face up to the nightmares of her past, if she is to discover what the future holds.

'WELCOME TO CLUB SKYLINE: ONE DOCTOR DICK'

For recently qualified Doctor, Scott Hunter, the burden of student debt weighs heavy on his mind.

But a chance meeting with the enigmatic yet charming and sexy club owner Alexander Alessio precedes an intriguing invite that could offer him his heart desires, but at what cost?

In a move that could risk his licence to practice, the lure of an exciting new world and the advantages of financial freedom and independence prove too strong a pull.

Welcome to Club Skyline-the most exclusive underground club in Liverpool, where every fetish is catered for, and every wish and desire fulfilled.

'ALONE'

"I shoulda been there—ride or die, Rox, ride or die."
With his marriage in tatters and the country struggling to emerge from the grips of the pandemic, ex-army mechanic Dallas McCall makes the biggest mistake of his life, resulting in many of his crew serving prison time.

Abandoned, he's left out in the cold—alone, with no wife or loyal brothers to fall back on.

With only one friend left in town, Dallas knows he lives on borrowed time, but scrambles to get enough cash together to leave Billings, Montana when a blast from the past re-enters his life begging for another chance.

Steadfast in his refusal to cast aside his own heartbreak, sending her into the night opens an opportunity for his unforgiving ex-crew members to exact revenge for what they view as the ultimate act of **betrayal**.

Acknowledgements

Angel Nevaeh – thank you for riding this amazing wave with me. You're the best.

Raven Canely & Cheryl Blackburn – your guidance is worth its weight in gold. Thank you!

Lara Luck – thank you for coordinating my Street Team. You totally rock, even when you have to kick my ass.

Dhani's Darling's. These wonderful women stepped in to help me out of the kindness of their hearts. I knew nothing and learn more every day, but I appreciate you all for taking me under the protective wings and helping me to fly. Thank you for everything!

To all who come to play in Dhani's Devilish Tongue – thank you for taking a chance on a new author.

And to the many authors and PA's who reached out to support me and invite me into your wonderful groups – your kindness is appreciated, and I hope one day I can be there when you need me.

My editing and formatting team. Thank you for shaping my work so I can present it as beautifully as possible.

Em - Thank you for taking my design idea and bringing it to life. The cover fits the story perfectly.

With love and gratitude

DHANI

X

About the Author

Dhani Ewing is a Best-Selling Author who was born and raised in Liverpool.

As an only child, he grew up with his single mother in a warm and loving environment. To this day, she remains his best friend.

Recently completing a medical degree, he travelled to America during his gap year, but was forced to return to England due to the global pandemic.

Once home, he set his mind to conquering a life-long dream of writing.

Finding immediate success with his debut novella, 'THE STRANGER', writing has now become a full-time hobby with many planned releases to follow.

As well as a burgeoning writing career, Dhani has started a three year core training course in psychiatry.

Life is busy but stay tuned... there is so much more to come!

www.ingramcontent.com/pod-product-compliance
Lightning Source LLC
Chambersburg PA
CBHW071520150726
48000CB00002B/614